I0670767

THE LOVE LIGHT OF APOLLO

Barbara Cartland

Barbara Cartland Ebooks Ltd

This edition © 2020

Copyright Cartland Promotions 1996

ISBNs

9781788673600   EPUB

9781788673617   PAPERBACK

Book design by M-Y Books

m-ybooks.co.uk

THE BARBARA CARTLAND ETERNAL COLLECTION

The Barbara Cartland Eternal Collection is the unique opportunity to collect all five hundred of the timeless beautiful romantic novels written by the world's most celebrated and enduring romantic author.

Named the Eternal Collection because Barbara's inspiring stories of pure love, just the same as love itself, the books will be published on the internet at the rate of four titles per month until all five hundred are available.

The Eternal Collection, classic pure romance available worldwide for all time .

THE LATE DAME BARBARA CARTLAND

Barbara Cartland, who sadly died in May 2000 at the grand age of ninety eight, remains one of the world's most famous romantic novelists. With worldwide sales of over one billion, her outstanding 723 books have been translated into thirty six different languages, to be enjoyed by readers of romance globally.

Writing her first book 'Jigsaw' at the age of 21, Barbara became an immediate bestseller. Building upon this initial success, she wrote continuously throughout her life, producing bestsellers for an astonishing 76 years. In addition to Barbara Cartland's legion of fans in the UK and across Europe, her books have always been immensely popular in the USA. In 1976 she achieved the unprecedented feat of having books at numbers 1 & 2 in the prestigious B. Dalton Bookseller bestsellers list.

Although she is often referred to as the 'Queen of Romance', Barbara Cartland also wrote several historical biographies, six autobiographies and numerous theatrical plays as well as books on life, love, health and cookery. Becoming one of Britain's most popular media personalities and dressed in her trademark pink, Barbara spoke on radio and television about social and political issues, as well as making many public appearances.

In 1991 she became a Dame of the Order of the British Empire for her contribution to literature and her work for humanitarian and charitable causes.

Known for her glamour, style, and vitality Barbara Cartland became a legend in her own lifetime. Best remembered for her wonderful romantic novels and loved by millions of readers worldwide, her books remain treasured for their heroic heroes, plucky heroines and traditional values. But above all, it was Barbara Cartland's overriding belief in the positive power of love to help, heal and improve the quality of life for everyone that made her truly unique.

AUTHOR'S NOTE

I fell in love with Greece when I first read *The Splendour of Greece* by Robert Payne.

When I went there, I found that this fascinating book answered so many questions and made me understand the mystery and beauty of the Ancient Gods.

Delos, where Apollo was born, is just as I have described it.

Some of the top Greek families are a part of my story, but the description of the Parthenon in the Erechtheion is exactly as I saw and felt it.

After 2,500 years Greece is still a mystical enigma to the Western World.

Just as Robert Payne puts it so clearly,

The splendour of Greece still lights our skies, reaching over America and Asia and lands which the Greeks never dream existed. There would be no Christianity as we know it without the fertilising influence of the Greek Fathers of the Church, who owed their training to Greek philosophy.

By a strange accident all the images of Buddha in the Far East can be traced right back to portraits of Alexander, who seemed to the Greeks to be Apollo incarnate.

We owe to the Greeks the beginning of science and the beginning of thought.

They built the loveliest Temples ever, carved marble with delicacy and strength and set in motion the questing mind which refuses to believe that there are any bounds to reason.

That is why we journey to Greece like pilgrims to a feast.

CHAPTER ONE
1874

"No! No! No! I will not do it —1 will *not*!" Princess Marigold's voice rose to a shriek on the last word.

Pulling off her slipper, she flung it as hard as she could at her Comptroller, Colonel Bassett, who was standing nearby

As this had happened to him before, he deftly side-stepped the missile.

The slipper landed on top of a cabinet, knocking over a pretty piece of antique Dresden china.

Princess Marigold was lying on the sofa and now she said in a slightly quieter voice,

"You can inform Her Majesty that I will not go to Greece and so that is the end of the matter!"

Colonel Bassett sighed and persevered.

"I am afraid, Your Royal Highness, that you cannot refuse a Royal Command from Her Majesty Queen Victoria."

"Why not?" Princess Marigold asked sharply. "This is supposed to be a free country."

Colonel Bassett did not reply and after a moment she carried on furiously,

"Free! Of course it is free for everyone, except someone like myself who is supposed to be Royal, but without a throne, and without anyone paying any attention to what I want or do not want to do!"

This again was something that Colonel Bassett had heard before and he remained silent.

Then unexpectedly the door opened and a voice came from it,

"Is anyone at home?"

The Princess sat up abruptly.

"Holden!" she exclaimed. "Thank Goodness you have come. What do you think has just happened?"

Prince Holden then came a little further into the room, nodded to Colonel Bassett and walked towards the Princess.

He was a tall, broad-shouldered and handsome young man but with somewhat Germanic features.

"I heard you shouting," the Prince said, "so I knew that there was trouble."

"Trouble!" Princess Marigold echoed. "Oh, Holden, Holden, what am I to do?"

The Prince took the Princess's hand and raised it to his lips.

"You are upsetting yourself, but you promised me that I should cope with your troubles and you would not become agitated over them."

"Agitated?" Princess Marigold exclaimed. "Of course I am agitated! Have you heard what that monstrous old woman here in Windsor Castle wants me to do?"

Prince Holden turned his head towards Colonel Bassett.

"What has happened?" he asked.

"Her Majesty," Colonel Bassett answered, speaking in a somewhat pompous voice, "has now informed Her Royal Highness that she is to represent Great Britain at the funeral of His Royal Highness Prince Eumenus of Malia."

"Oh, is he dead?" Prince Holden replied. "I had heard that he was ill."

"His Royal Highness is dead and his body has been embalmed so that he can be buried in Athens in two weeks' time," the Colonel went on. "While he was not of any great Diplomatic importance, Her Majesty feels that she personally and so, of course, Great Britain, should be represented at the Ceremony."

Prince Holden had been listening attentively.

Now he said quietly as he turned towards the Princess,

"You will have to go, my dearest."

"And leave you?" Princess Marigold exclaimed. "Can you not see what Queen Victoria is up to? She has never approved of our engagement and now she is doing everything in her power to separate us!"

"She will never do that," Prince Holden averred.

At the same time there was an anxious expression in his eyes.

After months of discussion Queen Victoria had finally allowed Princess Marigold, who was a near relation, to become engaged to Prince Holden of Allenberg.

No one could pretend that it was a marriage of prestige for the Princess.

But she had fallen madly in love with Prince Holden and she firmly refused to consider any other man who might be suggested to her.

Ever since she had been small, Princess Marigold had been what Queen Victoria thought of as a problem.

She had arrived to live in England with her father and mother after Prince Dimitri had been thrown out of Panaeros in a revolution.

It was a smallish Greek island where his family had reigned as Monarchs for generations.

Queen Victoria had, however, found the family a burden on her hands.

At first Prince Dimitri had begged Her Majesty over and over again to send British ships and British guns to restore him to his Throne by force if necessary.

When she refused to do so and he died, his wife Helen, who was English and a cousin of the Queen, had died of a broken heart.

In fact she had never forgiven Queen Victoria for refusing her husband's heart rendering request.

It was whispered amongst the Courtiers at Windsor Castle that she had put a Greek curse on the Queen before she herself had died.

Whether this was true or not, she had certainly left Her Majesty a considerable bundle of trouble in the shape of her only child.

The Princess had been christened 'Mary Gloriana Amethyst Victoria'.

The names had been chosen as compliments to her grandparents, her Godmothers and, of course, the Queen of Great Britain.

As soon as she could talk, Princess Mary, as it had been decided she should be called, refused to answer to any other name except that of 'Marigold'.

No one quite understood why it had taken her fancy and yet she insisted over and over again to her Nannies, her Governesses and anyone else who would listen, that her name was 'Marigold'.

It became impossible to call a child by her real name who would not answer to anything but the name that she had chosen for herself.

First her Nannies gave in to her whim, then her Governesses and Tutors.

Finally through sheer exasperation, Queen Victoria herself gave in as well.

Princess Marigold she then became and was undoubtedly a major thorn in the flesh of her benefactress.

She was brought up at Windsor Castle and indeed there was plenty of room in that huge unwieldy edifice for a dozen or more children if necessary.

But it was often felt by those in attendance that it was too small for Princess Marigold and she was invariably in trouble of one sort or another.

However, as she grew up, she became extremely pretty, in fact a real beauty.

She resembled her mother with her fair hair and pink-and-white English complexion. But her eyes were definitely Greek, dark, expressive and stunningly beautiful in their depths.

The combination was just so striking that whoever saw her looked at her and then looked at her again.

This made Queen Victoria even more determined to marry off Princess Marigold as soon as it was possible.

It would certainly mean a quieter and less turbulent atmosphere inside Windsor Castle.

Her Majesty might have known, however, that anyone she did chose for her troublesome relative would be totally unacceptable to her.

Usually before Princess Marigold had even seen the man in question she decided that she would not marry him. Crown Princes were suggested to her one after another.

All of whom were, as Queen Victoria knew, only too eager to be more closely associated with Great Britain and her ever-growing Empire.

Princess Marigold stamped her foot and cried, "No! No! *No!*"

Princes were invited to England and they came cocky and very pleased with themselves, confident that they would go home closely united through marriage to the British Throne.

They left with their tails between their legs.

A sharp little voice said, "no! no! no!" to everything they suggested.

Then unexpectedly and without any scheming by Queen Victoria, in fact it was without her knowledge, Princess Marigold met Prince Holden of Allenberg.

He had come to England to stay with some friends of his, who had studied at the same University.

His visit had not been notified as a special Royal Occasion to Buckingham Palace nor to Windsor Castle.

It was just by chance that Princess Marigold, having nothing at all to do one afternoon, thought that she would go to Ranelagh and watch the Polo.

She had been invited many times, but generally found that it was rather boring for the spectators. A lot of galloping about after a small ball.

However, when she looked in her diary, she found that there was nothing specific for her to do that day.

So she decided on an impulse that she would drive to Ranelagh.

A good-looking young Duke with whom she had danced the previous night had told her that he was playing against a team arranged by the German Embassy.

"I believe they rather fancy themselves," he had said, "but I am quite certain, Your Royal Highness, that we will win. We are in tip-top form and have won every game we have played so far this Season."

He had paused and then added,

"We would, of course, be very honoured if you would come to watch us play tomorrow afternoon."

Princess Marigold had actually enjoyed herself that evening. No one had pestered her to go home early or told her that she could not dance for the third time with the same partner.

She had therefore given orders when she awoke that she would be going to Ranelagh.

This meant that she had to take a Lady-in-Waiting with her.

The one whose turn it was complained bitterly,

"I have a headache," she told the other Ladies-in-Waiting. "So why cannot that tiresome girl stay here instead of gallivanting off to watch Polo where I will doubtless have to sit in the sun all afternoon."

She gave a sigh before continuing,

"I shall then have to listen to her saying all the way home that she was bored."

It must have been a real surprise to her later that Princess Marigold was in such a good temper.

Especially as, when they finally did drive back to Windsor Castle, it was quite late in the evening.

"I must see you tomorrow," Prince Holden had said as he helped her into her carriage.

"You will not forget?" the Princess had replied in a soft voice.

"How could you imagine that I could forget anything that concerns you?" he asked.

They had looked into each other's eyes.

It was with the greatest reluctance that the Prince moved away so that the footman could close the door of the carriage.

As Princess Marigold drove off, she bent forward to wave to him.

He then stood watching until the carriage was well out of sight.

*

Prince Holden had arrived at Windsor Castle the next day to pay his humble respects to Queen Victoria.

And she had received him in her study without much enthusiasm.

Allenberg was a very small South German Principality and of no particular importance or standing in the world.

However Her Majesty was determined to prevent the unscrupulous way that the Russians were trying to exert influence in a number of the smaller Balkan States.

They had already infiltrated into Serbia and the other North Balkan States as well.

The Czar of Russia had fortunately not been successful in gaining control of Bulgaria.

Prince Alexander of Battenberg had refused to act as a Russian puppet.

Finally the Russians kidnapped the Prince and had then forced him to abdicate at pistol-point.

Queen Victoria had been furious.

"Russia behaves and has behaved shamefully and disgracefully!" she raged.

It was because of what had happened in Bulgaria that finally she became more amenable to the idea of Princess Marigold marrying Prince Holden.

However Bulgaria was a large country while Allenberg was a very small one.

Over and over again she told Princess Marigold how advantageous it would be for her to marry a man who could make her a Queen.

To Queen Victoria's surprise, however, for almost the first time since the death of the Prince Consort, she found that she could not have her own way.

"I intend, Cousin Victoria," Princess Marigold insisted firmly, "to marry Prince Holden even if I have to elope with him and am never allowed to set foot on English soil again!"

Finally and reluctantly, because nothing she could say would move Princess Marigold, Queen Victoria conceded.

The engagement between Prince Holden of Allenberg and the Princess Maigold was to be announced the following week.

Unfortunately the day before the engagement should have appeared in the newspapers, an elderly relative of the Queen and the Princess had died unexpectedly.

This meant that Royalty were now to be dressed in black for six months and there was no question of even a minor Royal Wedding taking place until the time of mourning was past.

The Queen therefore decided that their engagement was to be kept secret from everyone except those living in Windsor Castle and the public announcement would be made when the actual date of the Wedding was decided.

Now in a voice that was almost hysterical Princess Marigold pointed out,

"Do you not understand, Holden, that Her Majesty will use the death of Prince Eumenus as an excuse to keep us in mourning."

She paused a moment to clear her throat before continuing,

"She is just hoping and praying that we will become bored with waiting and then she can marry me off to some doddering old King whose Throne is crumbling from under him!"

Prince Holden put his hand over the Princess's.

"We have a little more than two months to go," he said, "and I cannot believe that Prince Eumenus who was of little consequence, could expect us to mourn for any longer than that."

"But I will not leave you and go to Greece," Princess Marigold retorted. "I know exactly how Her Majesty's mind works. She is thinking that because Papa was Greek, I might find someone there of more importance than you."

Prince Holden was well aware that this was true.

But, as there was nothing more he could say, he raised the Princess's hand to his lips.

"Also," the Princess went on, "you promised that you would take me away in your yacht. I have not yet told the Queen, but I have decided who we would take with us as a chaperone, old Lady Milne."

She smiled at him and then carried on,

"If we give her enough to drink, she will sleep all through the afternoon and evening and not interfere with us at all."

"No one shall ever do that," the Prince asserted firmly.

"But that is exactly what the Queen is trying to do," the Princess said.

Now the anger was back in her voice.

"Surely there is someone else who would be able to go to Greece?" Prince Holden said turning to Colonel Bassett.

He was still standing somewhat uncomfortably by the door.

He was used to Princess Marigold's tantrums. Yet he could never make up his mind if it was best to leave the room without permission or to stay and witness her performance.

If he did stay, he would have to listen to her raging endlessly at him or anyone else who might have antagonised her.

"Even if there was, Your Royal Highness," he replied in answer to the Prince, "I doubt if Her Majesty would change her mind and send someone else in place of Her Royal Highness."

"Nevertheless you had better find someone," Princess Marigold said sharply. "For I am not going, even if I have to stay in bed and claim I am too ill to travel."

"I do so want you to be with me," Prince Holden said in a low caressing tone. "I was so looking forward to taking you across the North Sea to Denmark or anywhere else you would prefer."

"And I want to be with you too," the Princess sighed.

She was looking up into his eyes and for a moment they forgot that Colonel Bassett was in the room.

"I want to stand on deck at night and gaze at the stars," the Princess said, "and I want to keep counting the days until we can be married."

"That is what I am doing," the Prince replied and his fingers tightened on hers.

"Then let's defy the Queen," Princess Marigold suggested, "and send someone else in my place. As long as there is someone in dismal black with a Union Jack hanging over their heads, no one will care whether I am there or not."

"I agree," the Prince smiled, "but I would really doubt if anyone would be brave enough to impersonate you and risk the terrible wrath of Her Majesty."

"There must be someone if we could only find her," Princess Marigold persisted. "Surely you know someone, Colonel Bassett?"

"I am afraid not, Your Royal Highness," the Colonel answered swiftly.

"Oh, how can you be so unhelpful?" the Princess turned on him. "I thought you were on my side."

"Your Highness is well aware," the Colonel said, "that if I encouraged you to intrigue against Her Majesty's orders, I would be dismissed instantly, if I was not taken to the Tower of London as a traitor!"

He spoke lightly,

At the same time both the Prince and Princess knew that there was a great deal of truth in what he was saying.

As if he thought that it was a mistake to continue with this line of conversation, Colonel Bassett asked,

"If Your Royal Highness will now excuse me, I have a great many letters that need my attention."

"Yes, yes, of course," the Princess responded.

The words had hardly left her lips before Colonel Bassett had turned and hurried from the room, closing the door behind him.

The Prince put his arms round the Princess and pulled her close against him.

"I love you," he breathed, "and it is an agony to think that you have to go away from me. I suppose I could make the excuse that I too wish to go to Greece to attend Prince Eumenus's funeral."

"The Queen will not believe that," the Princess said, "because the other night, when she mentioned to you that he was feeling ill, you said quite positively that you had never ever heard of him."

The Prince sighed.

"I remember that now and I cannot think why I did not keep my mouth shut!"

"It is the sort of thing Her Majesty would remember," Princess Marigold said. "Anyway, I am sure that she would not allow you to travel with me, I suppose in a Battleship, unless they are being measly and sending me by train."

"If you are representing Her Majesty, then you will go by sea."

Being of German origin he was extremely knowledgeable on protocol.

And the Princess was sure that he was right.

"But I want to be with you, darling Holden," she insisted. "In your yacht and away from everyone including all these ghastly old fuddy-duddies, who keep on saying that I should not marry you."

"I am terrified in case you ever agree with them," the Prince commented.

"You know I would never, never do so!" the Princess answered. "I love you, Holden, and I had never loved anyone until I met you."

He pulled her into his arms and kissed her passionately until they were both breathless.

If the Queen had found out that the Princess received Prince Holden in her apartments without being chaperoned by a Lady-in-Waiting, she would have been outraged.

They were both aware that it was lucky that Prince Holden had come to find her when she was with her Comptroller.

It was Colonel Bassett who had suggested in the first place that it would be best for him to see the Princess alone in the mornings. Otherwise she would have her two aged and very garrulous Ladies-in-Waiting with her.

Now they could discuss privately plans on which they had not yet made a final decision without it being talked about all over Windsor Castle.

It had therefore been a golden opportunity for Prince Holden to be alone with Princess Marigold.

This was something with great difficulty that they were continually trying to find in The Castle.

Because the Queen disapproved of the engagement, she deliberately put every obstacle in their way.

Now, as the Prince raised his head, he said in a voice that was slightly unsteady,

"I love you, my dearest! I love you and I know that once we are married, we will be very happy. But I find this waiting just intolerable."

"So do I," the Princess said, "and it will be worse still when I have to go away. I suppose it will take a fortnight or even three weeks to go to Greece, attend the funeral, make myself agreeable to a whole collection of boring people and then come slowly home."

She gave an exclamation of anger as she addrd,

"I am sure that ghastly old woman will tell the ship's Captain to move at one knot per hour, just so that I cannot be with you!"

"You are not to upset yourself, darling. I swear that we will be married the very day the six months of mourning ends."

"If she will let us," the Princess murmured.

She gave a sudden cry.

"Suppose, just suppose, Holden, while I am away, she somehow gets rid of you? I would not trust her not to have you kidnapped or sent to Outer Mongolia or darkest Africa or some such place!"

Prince Holden laughed.

"Now you are just imagining things. I promise I will keep very quiet and out of sight, so as not to annoy Her Majesty, until you return."

"I will not go! I swear I will not go!" Princess Marigold cried. "There must be someone who can go in my place! Think, Holden, think! Who do we know who looks like me?"

As this was something that they had not thought of before, the Prince stared at her.

Then he remarked,

"It is rather funny that you should say that! I saw a girl last week who was in fact very like you."

"Was she a relative of mine?" Princess Marigold asked.

"I was staying with the Duke of Ilchester," the Prince went on, "and I went to Church on Sunday because the Duchess asked me rather pointedly, I thought, to escort her."

"Yes, yes, go on!" the Princess urged him.

"It was a pleasant village Service. But I was surprised to see in the Church in the front pew, sitting beside an attractive lady, a girl who might actually have been your sister."

"I don't believe it!" Princess Marigold exclaimed. "Who is she?"

"I asked the Duchess afterwards and she told me that the lady was the Vicar's wife and she was Greek."

"Greek?" the Princess exclaimed. "And the girl who looked like me?"

"Her daughter, named Avila, I was informed. I meant to tell you all about it, but I forgot until just now."

He smiled before he added,

"How can I think of anyone except for you?"

"If she looks like me," Princess Marigold said, "and, if she has some Greek blood in her, then let us offer to pay her, although, of course, we can put it more politely as a gift, to go to Greece in my place."

The Prince laughed.

"Now you are Fairy tailing again! I cannot believe for a moment she would be allowed to go or that she could take your place without anyone being aware of it."

"Then if she takes my place just before I am supposed to step aboard the ship, draped of course in black and her face obscured by a crêpe veil, who is to know?"

"Are you really serious?" Prince Holden asked. "You must be aware that the whole idea is crazy! The Queen would be absolutely furious if she learns of it."

"*If* she learns of it!" the Princess emphasised. "Now, Holden, we have to be clever about this. I know how brilliant you are at organisation. Surely you can organise this for me?"

She paused for a moment before she went on firmly,

"I love you! I love you! To be away from you even for a day is agony. To be gone from you for weeks I think would kill me!"

"My darling, my sweet, how can you say such things?" the Prince asked.

He pulled her close to him.

He would have kissed her again, but the Princess put her fingers over his lips.

"Promise me," she pleaded, "that you will try really hard to make it possible for me to come with you in your yacht. Promise me."

The Prince looked down at her and was lost.

Finally he said,

"I promise, but – "

Whatever he would have said was lost as Princess Marigold was kissing him wildly.

CHAPTER TWO

Driving his chaise with Princess Marigold beside him, Prince Holden related,

"We have escaped for the moment and it was just luck that I sat next to the Duchess of Ilchester at dinner last night."

"I think Fate is on our side," the Princess replied, "and now we have to persuade this Greek woman that it is advantageous for her daughter to go to Athens in my place."

The Prince looked serious.

He was thinking privately that it was very unlikely that the Vicar's wife would agree to anything quite so extraordinary.

What was more, he was certain that their plot would be discovered and Queen Victoria would be furious with them both.

However he knew better than to say so at this particular moment.

As they drove on, Princess Marigold commented,

"It will be wonderful to get away from everything in your yacht. You will have to plan it all out very carefully so that I leave at the same time as the girl goes to Athens."

Because he was so enjoying being alone with the Princess, Prince Holden did not argue about it and so made no reply.

He had very cleverly arranged that the Lady-in-Waiting should travel in another chaise behind them.

"I am so sorry," he had said, "but there really is not enough room for three people in the front of this chaise and so I cannot imagine that anyone would want to sit behind us with the groom."

Because they had left Windsor Castle very early in the morning, there were no Senior Officials about and they had driven off as the Prince had arranged.

The Lady-in-Waiting, Lady Bedstone, came behind them.

The Princess had chosen her carefully because she was old, slightly deaf and delighted to be going to luncheon with the Duke and Duchess of Ilchester.

"I told the Duchess," the Prince said when he was explaining to the Princess what he had arranged, "that you were longing to see her garden, which I had told you was very beautiful and you also wished to meet and have a talk with the Vicar's wife if that was at all possible."

"Was she surprised?" Princess Marigold enquired.

"She was, until I explained that no one in The Castle was Greek and the few who spoke the language did so, in your opinion, very badly."

"If everything goes the way you have planned it, it will be wonderful!" the Princess said.

She had no idea that Prince Holden had lain awake all through tha night wondering how he could persuade her to change her mind.

He finally decided that he would rely on the Vicar's wife. He was sure that she would refuse to allow her daughter to take part in a lie by pretending to be the Princess.

Princess Marigold was thrilled, however, at the way everything was going.

She put her hand on the Prince's knee as she sighed,

"I love you, Holden, and I swear to you that nothing and nobody shall stop us from being married the very day I am out of mourning."

"If all else fails," the Prince said blithely, "we will run away together. We can be married in France or anywhere else we go. Then Her Majesty, however important she may be, can do nothing about it whatsoever."

"I would expect that she will think up some outlandish punishment," Princess Marigold groaned. "But she will not be able to prevent me from becoming your wife."

"No one can prevent it!" the Prince asserted.

He was, like Princess Marigold, head-over-heels in love.

He realised, of course, that it would indeed be of tremendous benefit to his Principality to be allied to the British Throne.

He had been attracted by a number of women in the past and they by him.

He had, however, never felt as he felt now. At the same time he was aware that he must keep his head.

He was trying to prevent Princess Marigold from doing something reckless that would incur the legendary wrath of Queen Victoria.

He was well aware that everyone was frightened of Her Majesty and intimidated by her including the Prince of Wales and his siblings.

He had thought at his first interview that she was the most awe-inspiring person he had ever met in the whole of his life.

He knew that his father would be extremely annoyed if the Queen turned her back on him and it would be a catastrophe if he and the Princess were not accepted at Windsor Castle in the future.

But the sun was shining and Princess Marigold loved him!

It seemed impossible at this very moment that the future could be dull and dismal for them both.

They reached the Duke's house, which was only about six miles from Windsor Castle.

He owned a number of other houses in the London area, but Chester Park was one of the most impressive.

Set in five-thousand acres of land, it had been in the family for centuries and it had been added to by a number of different generations.

As they drove up the drive, Prince Holden thought that it was more of a Palace than a country house.

The Duchess greeted Princess Marigold affectionately, exclaiming as they entered the drawing room,

"It is delightful to see Your Royal Highness and such a lovely surprise."

"I know your garden is beautiful," the Princess replied, "and, as I had nothing dull and formal to do today, it was a perfect opportunity to come here with Prince Holden."

The Prince bowed and then kissed the Duchess's hand.

When the Duke joined them, they went into the dining room for luncheon.

Half-way through the meal the Duchess declared to Princess Marigold,

"Prince Holden tells me that you wish to speak with Mrs. Grandell, who is Greek."

"I would love to do so, if it is not too much trouble," Princess Marigold replied. "I am so frightened that now that Papa and Mama are dead I shall forget my Greek and have to learn it from a book, which is never the same as speaking the language with a native."

"I am sure that is true," the Duchess agreed, "and I have sent a message to Mrs. Grandell telling her that you, ma'am, would call on her at about three o'clock this afternoon."

"That is very kind of you," the Princess smiled. "Do tell me, where does she come from in Greece?"

It seemed to her that the Duchess was suddenly at a loss for words.

She looked across the table at her husband, who said quickly,

"Mrs. Grandell is a very reserved woman and seldom talks to anyone about Greece or the time when she left the country."

The Duke then went on to discuss with Prince Holden some new horses that he had just bought and how pleased he was with them.

The conversation about Mrs. Grandell thus came to an abrupt end.

Princess Marigold, who was very quick-witted, guessed that there was some secret and it was something that she was not meant to find out and she wondered what it could possibly be.

She managed, however, to be extremely interested in the garden, which she was shown around after luncheon.

But she was really counting the minutes until they could leave the Duke's house.

As they drove down the drive with Lady Bedstone following them, the Princess heaved a deep sigh of relief.

"I have never known time pass so slowly," she complained to Prince Holden.

"You must not be disappointed, my darling," he told her, "if Mrs. Grandell will not agree to what you suggest and then we will have to try and find somebody else."

"I cannot imagine that there are many others in the world who look exactly like me," the Princess replied.

"Maybe I was mistaken," Prince Holden said a little uncomfortably. "After all I only saw the girl in Church."

"We will soon know whether you are right or wrong," the Prince said as he drew up his chaise at the front door of the Vicarage.

The Princess had been sensible enough to tell Lady Bedstone that it would be a mistake for her to come into the Vicarage with them.

"The Duchess said," she told her when they were alone for just a moment, "that Mrs. Grandell is very reserved. I am sure therefore that you will understand when I ask you to wait outside."

"I would much rather do that, ma'am," Lady Bedstone replied. "I find getting in and out of carriages very tiring. And it was so hot walking round the garden."

"Then you must rest in the shade," the Princess said in a comforting tone. "We will not be long."

The Vicar, the Reverend Patrick Grandell, was waiting for them with the front door open when they climbed out of the chaise.

He gave a very correct bow to the Princess as to Royalty, moving only his head and not his shoulders and he did the same to the Prince, who shook him warmly by the hand.

"My wife is waiting for you, ma'am, in the drawing room," he related to the Princess. "I thought perhaps that His Royal Highness would like to come and look at my bowling green, which I have just completed, and also a target I have just erected for an archery contest."

"I would very much like to see them both," the Prince agreed.

The Vicar led him away across a small hall and opened a door on the other side of it.

"Her Royal Highness is here, Lycia," he called out.

His wife, who had been sitting sewing in the window, hastily rose to her feet.

The girl who was sitting beside her rose as well.

When Princess Marigold looked at her, she gave a little gasp.

There was no doubt that the Prince was right.

Although it seemed so extraordinary, the daughter of the Vicar and his wife were indeed very much like her.

She had the same fair hair, which was very understandable as the Vicar himself was fair-haired and blue-eyed.

But she had her mother's dark Greek eyes that seemed to be almost too big for her small pointed face.

She was just so like the Princess that it was uncanny.

She was, however, two years younger and there was something about Avila's beauty that the Princess did not have.

There was, Prince Holden thought, something essentially spiritual about her.

Something which made her seem not quite human, as if she belonged to a different world from that of other people.

As the Vicar's wife curtseyed very gracefully, her daughter did the same.

Then the Vicar said in a jovial manner,

"His Royal Highness and I are going to leave you, Lycia. I was never a particularly good linguist where Greek is concerned and I rather suspect His Royal Highness finds it a difficult language to follow."

"I am afraid it's the truth," Prince Holden agreed. "My French and Italian are far better."

The Vicar laughed and then closed the door behind them

Mrs. Grandell then said politely in Greek,

"Would Your Royal Highness like to sit in the sunshine or would you find it cooler on the sofa?"

She indicated a sofa near the fireplace and the Princess moved towards it.

When she had sat down, she said in a low voice,

"I have come to ask you for your help, Mrs. Grandell, and please do help me, because it is very very important for me."

Mrs. Grandell, who was, the Princess decided, a beautiful woman with an unmistakable dignity about her, responded in surprise,

"Of course! I should be delighted to help Your Royal Highness, if it is at all possible."

As if she thought that she might be intruding, Avila began to walk towards the door.

"No, no, please stop," Princess Marigold urged her. "I want you to hear what I have to say because it concerns you."

Avila looked a little bewildered, but she sat down in a chair beside her mother's.

Quickly, because she felt that she might not have too much time left before the Vicar returned, Princess Marigold then told Mrs. Grandell how she had fallen in love with Prince Holden.

She explained how on the very day that their engagement was to have been announced, they had been plunged into mourning.

"I will be frank with you," she said, "and explain that I am terrified, because Her Majesty the Queen wants me to marry someone very important, that she will use any excuse to try to separate us."

Mrs. Grandell was listening with an astonished expression in her eyes.

"But, surely – ?" she began.

"Allow me to finish please," the Princess interrupted. "You may have heard of Prince Eumenus of Malia, who has just died. He is to be buried in Athens and his body is being embalmed in order to give the prestigious people of Europe time to attend the Ceremony."

Princess Marigold had been watching Mrs. Grandell as she spoke.

She thought that there was a flicker in her eyes which told her that she knew who Prince Eumenus was.

"Malia is, I believe, only a small island, but Queen Victoria has decided I must represent her at the funeral of this Prince."

"Surely," Mrs. Grandell said a little tentatively, "Her Majesty could find someone older than Your Royal Highness for what is inevitably a somewhat gloomy occasion?"

"She could, but she will not," Princess Marigold replied, "simply because she wishes to separate me from Prince Holden."

She clasped her hands together as she went on,

"But I have fallen in love. I love him so much, Mrs. Grandell, as only you who are Greek can understand. If we are separated, as Her Majesty is trying to do, I think it would kill me!"

She was speaking from her heart. Her voice seemed to vibrate across the small room.

"I understand what you are feeling," Mrs. Grandell said quietly, "but I don't know how I can help you."

"What I am asking," Princess Marigold said, "is if your daughter Avila will go to Athens for the funeral in my place."

Mrs. Grandell stared at the Princess as if she could not believe what she was hearing.

Avila gave a little cry.

"Are you suggesting, ma'am, that I could go to Greece?" she asked. "It is something I have always longed to do ever since I was a small child."

"I am asking you to impersonate me and go to Athens," the Princess said, "and to see, despite the funeral Ceremony, as much of Greece as you can in the time available."

"This is the most wonderful thing that could possibly happen to me!" Avila cried.

Mrs. Grandell seemed at last to find her voice.

"Are you really serious, ma'am?" she enquired. "I can hardly believe what Your Royal Highness is saying."

"I am saying that I am desperate! I know that, if I go to Greece and leave Prince Holden, Her Majesty will somehow or other prevent our marriage from taking place or at least delay it in some tricky way of her own."

She drew in her breath and then went on,

"Please, please let Avila go instead of me. We look so alike that I am quite certain no one will have the slightest idea that she is not actually me."

Mrs. Grandell turned to look at her daughter and then back again at the Princess.

"There is indeed a definite – resemblance," she admitted slowly.

"If we were not side by side, no one would doubt for a moment that Avila is me," the Princess said quickly. "I think that we must be related in some way, as so many Greeks are."

To her surprise Mrs. Grandell stiffened.

"That, ma'am," she said, "is something I would not wish to discuss. I admit that there is a resemblance, but I am sure that my husband would not allow Avila to act a lie."

"Then you must not tell him," the Princess said. "As a Greek, you understand what I am feeling as no woman of any other nationality could. I can only beg you and plead with you to help me because this concerns my whole happiness, now and for the future."

"I don't know what to say," Mrs. Grandell murmured.

She had not moved or fidgeted while the Princess was talking and now she clasped her hands together almost as if they helped her to control her feelings.

"Oh, please, Mama, please!" Avila begged her. "Let me go to Greece! You know how thrilled I have been by the stories you have told me ever since I was a baby and the books we have read and the pictures we have found together."

She stopped for a moment before she went on,

"I never thought I would be able to see the Parthenon or any of the islands that you have told me so many stories about. Please, Mama please! Let me do what Her Royal Highness asks."

Princess Marigold felt that the girl's pleading was even more impressive than her own.

Then, still speaking Greek, Mrs. Grandell asked,

"Will you tell me, Your Royal Highness, how you think you can manage this deception without anyone being – aware of it?"

Princess Marigold felt her heart leap.

"I will tell you what I have discussed so far with Prince Holden," she said, "and, as he is a marvellous organiser, he will work out every detail so that there is not the slightest chance of our being discovered."

She saw that the Mrs. Grandell was still undecided and so she went on persuadingly,

"You must tell your husband that Avila is coming to Greece with me, which is almost true. Tell him I am taking her with me because, having lived in. England for so long, I must practise my Greek and be certain that I don't make any silly mistakes when I reach Athens."

She thought as she spoke that Mrs. Grandell thought that this sounded at least a possible idea.

"It is quite true," she continued, "there is nobody at Windsor Castle who I can converse with in Greek and I have in fact become rather rusty since my father and mother died. It was, of course, my father who taught me first when I was a child to speak in Greek."

"I am sure that Papa would think it a wonderful opportunity," Avila persisted, "for me to go to Greece and be Your Royal Highness for a while."

"You will travel by ship," Princess Marigold said, "and I will choose a Lady-in-Waiting to accompany you who is getting old and also rather blind."

She stopped speaking for a moment and then resumed,

"She will, I expect, be the only other English person in the party with the exception of the Under Secretary of State for Foreign Affairs, whom I have never met."

She gave a little laugh as she added,

"I am sure that they will expect me to remain in my cabin and feel sea-sick all through the Bay of Biscay and, when the ship reaches Athens, neither our Ambassador there nor any of his staff have ever met me."

Princess Marigold coughed and then carried on,

"This is all a plot of Queen Victoria's to try to separate us. I am certain that she is at this very moment working out in her mind how I will forget him and he will forget me. But that is something that will never ever happen!"

Now the anxious note was back in her voice.

There was something very pathetic in her eyes as she added,

"Please, please help me! There is no one else who I can turn to and only someone who is Greek can understand what I feel."

Avila looked at her mother.

Then, as Mrs. Grandell did not speak, she put a hand over hers.

"Please, Mama, please," she begged. "We would be very careful not to upset Papa and I promise I will do everything Her Royal Highness tells me to do."

"You just have to smile, keep saying 'thank you', and wave to the crowds," the Princess said. "I can assure you, being a Royal person requires no brains, not unless you are in a spot like me and have to try to save yourself."

Mrs. Grandell now realised that both the Princess and her daughter were looking at her pleadingly.

In a strange tone that did not sound like her usual voice, she said,

"As I would like Avila to see Greece and because I am aware of the strange resemblance there is between her and Your Royal Highness, I will agree. But the only condition is that this is kept completely secret and my husband is not made aware of what is happening."

"I can assure you that from my point of view," Princess Marigold answered, "no one will know except for us three and, of course, Prince Holden."

She smiled and then went on,

"I will rely on him to work out every single move and every tiny detail so that we are not discovered."

Mrs. Grandell did not speak and the Princess added as an afterthought,

"Avila and I are almost the same size and all that she will require is that dismal boring black of which I have dozens and dozens of gowns! Besides, of course, the correct bonnet with a dark veil which will prevent anyone from looking too closely at her until she is aboard the Battleship."

"And I can keep my head bent," Avila suggested, "as if it is such a moving occasion that I must not look too happy about it."

The Princess smiled.

"Exactly. I am sure that you will act the part very well and be much more charming and good-tempered than I would be."

She gave a little laugh and went on,

"And I would be hating every minute of the voyage, the funeral and the people who are preventing me from being with Prince Holden."

"While I will love every minute of it," Avila said in a rapt voice. "Oh, thank you, thank you, Your Royal Highness, for thinking of me."

"You should really thank Prince Holden, who happened to see you in Church," Princess Marigold said. "But be very careful what you say to him if he is with your father."

"So you are not to say anything at all," Mrs. Grandell came in. "The sole reason, Your Royal Highness, that I am allowing Avila to go on what seems to me a rather dangerous and certainly unusual journey is that she has always longed to see Greece."

She smiled and then added reflectively,

"It was my country and I have wanted her to see it too. There is nowhere in the world that can compare with that sublime country."

"That is what my father always said," Princess Marigold agreed, "and it broke his heart when the revolutionaries took away his Throne."

"I suppose they were incited to rebel by the Russians," Mrs. Grandell said. "They have caused trouble in so many of the Balkan States. I have heard recently that they have also been busy in Greece."

Princess Marigold had heard Queen Victoria's views on Russia's recent behaviour, but she felt it unnecessary to become involved in that discussion at the moment.

Instead she said,

"I know that Avila will love Greece and I expect you have told her many stories about it that she will feel as if she is going home rather than to a foreign country."

For the first time since they had started their conversation, Mrs. Grandell smiled at the Princess.

"You understand," she replied softly.

"As Greeks," the Princess said, "we both know it is important for Avila to see Greece and how better than being taken to everything that she asks to see because they believe she is me?"

"That is exactly what I was thinking," Mrs. Grandell nodded. "Yet I can only pray, Your Royal Highness, that our little plot will not be discovered. Because if it is, there will be a great number of people very angry with us."

"No one is more aware of that than I am," the Princess agreed. "I assure you, I shall be extremely careful and will not be happy until the Battleship moves out of Port carrying Avila instead of me!"

Avila clasped her hands together.

"Oh, thank you, thank you, ma'am!" she cried. "How can I ever tell you how grateful I am for this wonderful opportunity?"

She looked so pretty as she spoke that the Princess could not help saying,

"How is it possible that we look so alike? Surely, Mrs. Grandell, you must be aware of some explanation for it?"

To her surprise Mrs. Grandell then rose to her feet.

"I think, Your Royal Highness, it would be a mistake to speak of anything except for the task that lies ahead. I have so much to teach Avila before she leaves and a lot to tell her about Athens which is the one part of Greece she will certainly see."

"You must see everything else you can," the Princess turned to Avila. "In a way I envy you. At the same time, even for the great splendour of Greece, I cannot risk losing my future happiness."

She rose from the sofa as she spoke and put out her hand towards Mrs. Grandell.

"Thank you for being so understanding. I knew as soon as Prince Holden said you were Greek not only that we shared the same language but also that we can understand each other without words."

It was a pretty speech, said with all the charm that Princess Marigold could use when she chose to do so and when she wanted something special and would not be denied it.

"Your Royal Highness is very kind," Mrs. Grandell said. "Avila and I will wait for your instructions and then carry them out to the letter."

"Thank you again," Princess Marigold smiled, "and now I must return to Windsor Castle to work out with Prince Holden every detail of what we have to do now."

"And when do you expect to leave?" Mrs. Grandell asked.

"On Thursday," Princess Marigold replied. "It will be from the Port of Tilbury and, of course, Prince Holden will send a carriage for you. I have not yet been told the name of the Battleship that I am supposed to be travelling in."

She saw the expression of delight in Avila's eyes as she spoke and said,

"That is something you will enjoy and naturally the Captain and the crew will be very proud to have been chosen to carry the Representative of Great Britain to Greece."

"I think I – must be – dreaming!" Avila stammered. "This cannot really be – happening to me!"

"It is," Princess Marigold assured her, "and when you listen to all the long and dreary speeches which those who welcome you will make, you will find it very difficult not to yawn or go to sleep!"

Avila laughed and it was a very pretty sound.

"I am sure, ma'am, you are always clever enough to look as if you are enjoying it all, however dull it may be."

"That is what I tell myself I should do," the Princess said, "but I warn you, old men can talk and talk for hours."

Both Mrs. Grandell and Avila were laughing at this when the door opened.

"May we come in?" the Vicar asked, "or are you still dreaming that you are living on Mount Olympus?"

"Of course that is where we are," Princess Marigold replied. "For who could doubt that your daughter and I are Goddesses?"

As she spoke, she saw the expression in Prince Holden's eyes and realised that was how she appeared to him.

She felt a surge of love sweep over her.

'Even if Queen Victoria discovers our plot and punishes me,' she told herself, 'it will be worth the risk if I can be with him!'

CHAPTER THREE

The Traveller's Rest at Tilbury was a hotel where the guests never stayed for very long.

People arriving by sea might stay there temporarily and travellers leaving in ships used it until they knew that they could go aboard.

No one took any notice of a lady who had engaged a room for herself and her daughter on Wednesday night.

She was noted in the Register as 'Mrs. Johnson'.

As soon as she and her daughter arrived, they went straight upstairs to their bedroom on the first floor and stayed there all night.

The following morning there was a rumble of excitement amongst those working in the hotel.

They knew that a party was arriving from Windsor Castle and they would require coffee in the Private Lounge.

At a quarter after ten the first smart carriage arrived and drove up the dusty road to the hotel.

In it was Princess Marigold and sitting beside her was Prince Holden. And opposite them were Lady Bedstone and Colonel Bassett.

"I absolutely refuse to go aboard and do all that hand-shaking until I have had a cup of coffee," Princess Marigold had insisted on the way.

"I thought that was what you would want," Prince Holden replied, "and I have already engaged a private room for you."

"The only other passengers, ma'am," Colonel Bassett then informed her, "will be Lord Cardiff, the Minister of State for Foreign Affairs, whom I don't think you have met and the Greek Ambassador, who I believe is a very charming gentleman."

"In which case," Princess Marigold pointed out strongly, "I wonder why I have not been allowed to meet him before."

There was no answer to that question and they drove on in silence until they reached *The Traveller's Rest.*

Prince Holden climbed out of the carriage and then helped the Princess to alight.

They were greeted by the somewhat flurried Manager of the hotel, who escorted them to a Private Lounge. The luggage had already left Windsor Castle before the Princess set off.

It had been arranged that she should have a Greek lady's maid, who was provided by the Greek Embassy.

There had been little surprise about this at Windsor Castle, but the Princess had insisted,

"I am not going to be in a position where I cannot send my maid for anything I require or which has been forgotten simply because she cannot speak the language."

She paused a moment after this assertion and then went on,

"If I am going to Greece, I need a Greek lady's maid and preferably one who knows the shops in Athens."

No one felt inclined to argue with her on this.

The coffee was ready on the table for the Royal party.

The Princess, who was wearing the deepest black with a bonnet from which hung a long chiffon veil, accepted one of the sandwiches that Prince Holden offered her.

Then she asked,

"At what time are we due aboard the Battleship?"

"The Captain wishes to sail at eleven o'clock," Prince Holden replied, "so I expect that Colonel Bassett has arranged for us to arrive on the quay at about a quarter to the hour."

"That is what I planned we would do," Colonel Bassett nodded.

Lady Bedstone was already taking pills with her coffee and Princess Marigold knew that she had received them from the doctor just before she left.

They were a preventative against sea-sickness, but she was certain that they would make Her Ladyship sleepy as well.

There had been further surprise among the ladies at Windsor Castle that Lady Bedstone had been chosen for the journey.

But the Princess explained that she had asked for Lady Bedstone as she was retiring at the end of the summer. She also thought that she would enjoy the rest during the voyage, both there and back.

No one could say that this gesture was not a kind thought and Lady Bedstone had been very touched.

"The Princess may often be difficult," she said to the other Ladies-in-Waiting, which was indeed an under-statement, "but at the same time she has a kind heart."

The Princess, having drunk a little of her coffee now said,

"I am going to go up the stairs to tidy myself. I believe you have engaged a room for me, Holden?"

"Yes, of course," the Prince replied. "I will find a maid to take you there."

They then went from the lounge together.

As the passage outside was deserted, Prince Holden kissed her hand.

"Don't you worry your pretty little head, my darling one," he whispered, "everything is going smoothly."

"Touch wood!" the Princess murmured.

The Prince went into the main hall and found a maid to take Her Royal Highness up the stairs.

The maid in a mobcap and a bright gingham dress hurriedly obeyed and the Princess was shown into a large double room.

"Be there anythin' Your Royal 'Ighness wants?" the maid enquired.

"No, thank you," the Princess replied, "and you need not wait. I can easily find my own way back downstairs."

The maid bobbed her a rather clumsy curtsey and went out of the room, closing the door behind her.

The Princess waited until she thought that she must be out of earshot.

Then, as Prince Holden had told her to do, she tapped on the wall on the right hand side of the room.

As she did so, she was praying that everything had gone according to plan and that Avila would be there waiting for her.

Two seconds later she slipped in through the door.

She was wearing a black gown that was very similar to the one the Princess had on. But she had no bonnet on her shining golden hair.

Her eyes were excited and she looked so pretty that for a moment Princess Marigold felt almost jealous of her.

Avila dropped a curtsey.

"Is everything all right, ma'am?" she asked.

"Everything so far," Princess Marigold answered rather nervously.

As she spoke, she took off the bonnet she was wearing and handed it to Avila.

It had been easy to provide her double with gowns, but she had only one black bonnet and she had been afraid that it would cause a good deal of comment if she ordered another.

Avila had arrived with her mother, wearing her ordinary clothes and a hat trimmed with flowers.

The only item she had added and, which had been her own idea, was a pair of spectacles and they had hidden the beauty of her eyes.

However, with so many people coming in and going out of the Hotel, nobody had taken any notice of either her or her mother.

Avila said now,

"I think I should tell Your Royal Highness that I wore the spectacles when I arrived and perhaps it would be a good idea, ma'am, for you to wear them when you leave."

"I will do that," Princess Marigold agreed, "and I hope your mother has one of my own gowns ready for me next door."

"Yes, ma'am, they arrived last night. We had just been praying that they had not been forgotten."

Avila went to the dressing table to adjust the bonnet on her head and pull the chiffon veil over her face.

"Do I look all right, ma'am?" she asked a little anxiously.

"You look exactly like me," the Princess assured her. "And don't forget when you go downstairs that you are feeling sad and upset at having to leave Prince Holden. Everyone will understand if you are not very talkative."

"Then – shall I go – now?" Avila asked as if she suddenly felt too helpless to make any decision herself.

The Princess glanced at the clock on the mantelpiece.

"In another three minutes and in case anyone comes into this room and sees us together, I will go and join your mother."

She put out her hand and laid it on Avila's shoulder.

"Thank you for doing this for me," she said. "I am very grateful and I hope you will have a lovely time in Greece."

Avila curtseyed and Princess Marigold went towards the door.

She opened it very cautiously and looked up and down the corridor. It was empty and she swiftly moved into the room next door.

Mrs. Grandell was waiting for her and had one of the Princess's own summer gowns laid out on the bed.

Her Majesty the Queen had not called for Court mourning for Prince Eumenus. He was not important enough for that.

But she had said that she expected relations and Ladies-in-Waiting to wear black on the day of the funeral.

Princess Marigold talked to Mrs. Grandell in Greek as she then helped her into her pretty gown.

Next she put on the hat that was decorated to match it.

By the time she was dressed it was a few minutes to eleven o'clock and she knew that by now the party downstairs would be going aboard the Battleship, *H.M.S. Heroic.*

The only person who she had been really nervous about was Colonel Bassett.

If he guessed at the very last minute that they were deceiving Queen Victoria, he might consider it his duty to inform Her Majesty of what they were doing.

Prince Holden had, however, thought of this.

Avila went up the gangway to be greeted with great respect by the Captain and three of his Officers.

She was followed first by the Prince and then by Lady Bedstone.

After her came Lord Cardiff and finally, bringing up the rear were Colonel Bassett and the Greek Ambassador.

By the time he was greeting the Captain, Prince Holden had taken the Princess down the companionway. A Steward then led them to the cabins which had been allotted to Her Royal Highness for the voyage.

There was the one where she was to sleep and the Greek lady's maid from the Embassy was already busy unpacking her gowns.

Next to it was what had been the Captain's day cabin. This had been hastily turned into a sitting room for the Royal Party.

When they reached it, Prince Holden remarked,

"I think, as those following us will suppose we are saying 'goodbye' to each other, there will be a slight delay before they join us."

He had left the door ajar and he looked back towards the companionway before he said,

"I think that I should now go back and take Colonel Bassett away before he asks to say 'goodbye' to you."

"That would be sensible," Avila replied, "and anyway I will now go into my bed cabin so that no one except Lady Bedstone will follow me."

"You are quite safe where she is concerned," the Prince said. "She cannot see without using her lorgnettes and invariably mislays them!"

Avila gave a little laugh before she praised him,

"I think all your arrangements have been marvellous and I am so excited to be here that I am more grateful than I can say."

"And we are both even more grateful to you," the Prince replied. "Take very good care of yourself and try not to be frightened by anyone or anything."

Avila smiled at him through her veil and, as they heard footsteps on the companionway, she slipped into her cabin.

She then began speaking in Greek to the maid, who was concentrating on hanging up her clothes.

The Prince went up above and he found, as he expected, that the Captain was waiting somewhat impatiently for him and Colonel Bassett to leave the Battleship.

Having shaken hands and wishing everyone a good voyage, the Prince hurried down the gangway.

There were two closed carriages waiting on the quay.

One was there to take Colonel Bassett back to Windsor Castle. And the Prince's carriage was standing just near it.

"I thought I might offer Your Royal Highness a lift,' Colonel Bassett said as he followed him down the gangway.

"As it happens, I am going in the opposite direction," Prince Holden replied, "but I will see you, of course, as soon as Her Royal Highness returns."

"I can only hope that the funeral is not as depressing as Her Royal Highness anticipates," Colonel Bassett answered.

"I hope so too," the Prince replied. "But you know only too well how these funerals are conducted and I am very grateful that I don't have to be one of the mourners."

Colonel Bassett agreed and the Prince walked away and climbed into his own carriage.

He deliberately waited some way from the hotel until Colonel Bassett had driven away and his carriage was well out of sight.

Then he drove back to *The Traveller's Rest,* where he saw a closed carriage waiting for Mrs. Grandell.

He opened the door of his own carriage to alight, but before he could do so Princess Marigold ran down the steps of the hotel and jumped in beside him.

As the Prince put out his hands towards her, the coachman, who already had his orders, drove off to a different quay.

It was quite some distance from the one where *H.M.S. Heroic* had been tied up.

The horses moved slowly through piles of luggage, people boarding other ships and a large number of new arrivals.

The Princess flung herself against Prince Holden.

"We have done it! *We have done it!*" she cried.

Because Prince Holden was as excited as she was, he did not answer.

He just drew her closer to him and then he kissed her.

Only when she could speak again did the Princess enthuse,

"How can you have been so incredibly clever? How can you have been so wonderful as to work out everything so perfectly?"

She paused before she asked in a different rather worried voice,

"No one on the ship was suspicious in any way?"

"No one," the Prince responded triumphantly.

"And Colonel Bassett?"

"He hardly had a chance to get near to Avila and did not speak even one word to her. He has gone back to Windsor Castle, pleased with himself that he was able to make the Princess accept the Queen's instructions more peacefully to go to Greece."

The Princess gave a little laugh.

Then she suggested nervously,

"Let's get away from here just as quickly as possible. I am so afraid that something will prevent us from doing so at the very last minute."

As she spoke, the horses came to a standstill.

She looked out of the window to see the Prince's yacht moored to the quay.

The Prince climbed out of the carriage first and then he helped the Princess to alight and escorted her up the gangway.

The Captain of the yacht was waiting for them and the Prince, who had seen him on the previous day, merely ordered,

"Put to sea immediately, Captain Bruce."

The Captain bowed and the Prince drew Princess Marigold into the Saloon.

The yacht was large and comfortable and the Saloon was attractively decorated, although with somewhat masculine taste.

There was a bottle of champagne waiting for them in a wine-cooler.

The Prince looked at Princess Marigold.

"Will you have a cup of coffee or a glass of champagne?" he asked her.

"Champagne, of course!" she answered. "We have so much to celebrate you and I."

"Yes, very very much to celebrate." the Prince repeated.

The way he spoke made her look at him quickly.

"What in particular?" she asked him directly.

"I will show you exactly what I mean after you have had a glass of champagne and we go below."

"Now you are being mysterious," Princess Marigold protested.

The Prince next poured out two full glasses of champagne.

Then, as Princes Marigold lifted her glass, she gave a little cry.

"We are moving! We are moving! Oh, Holden, we have done it! We have escaped and now we can really enjoy ourselves without a boring Lady-in-Waiting always watching us. And without the dreary elderly Statesmen, the endless Politicians and without, of course, the watchful eye of Her Majesty the Queen!"

She put down her glass of champagne for a moment and pulling off her hat threw it onto a chair.

"We are free! We are free for two weeks or more," she cried, "and I want them to be the happiest days you have ever spent."

"I have made very sure of that" the Prince replied.

There was a distinct intonation in the way he spoke which made the Princess look at him questioningly.

"Drink your champagne," he prompted. "I have something to show you."

"You are making me more and more curious," the Princess complained. "I only hope it is not a surprise that will frighten me."

"I would certainly hope not," the Prince smiled.

Princess Marigold then finished her glass of champagne and by this time, the yacht was moving out of the quay and into the estuary.

The sun was shining brightly and shimmering on the sea and for a moment she just stood gazing out of one of the portholes in the Saloon.

Then she said,

"You have not yet told me where we are going."

"I want you to believe it is to Heaven," the Prince replied. "Now come and see what I have to show you."

Mystified, the Princess took his hand and they went down the companionway together.

The yacht was a new model and equipped with all the latest devices and new inventions from America.

They began to walk towards the stern of the yacht where Princess Marigold knew that the Master cabin would be located.

She thought questioningly that there was a serious expression in the Prince's eyes.

'Surely nothing can have gone wrong?' she asked herself.

Suddenly she was afraid in case he had brought someone else with them.

She knew if he had done so that it would spoil all her joy at being alone with him.

The Prince then opened the door of the Master cabin.

There was a large bed which traditionally was a four-poster draped with curtains.

There was, however, no one in the cabin and, as she had been afraid that there might be, the Princess gave a sigh of relief.

Then she was aware that lying on the bed there was a large bouquet of white flowers and beside it there was a huge wreath of white orchids.

She looked at them and then she asked him,

"Are all these for me?"

"They are for my bride," the Prince answered.

The Princess stared at him.

"We are being married, my darling," he said, "just as soon as we are further out to sea. It will be a Marriage performed by my Captain, which is entirely legal and no one can ever take you from me."

For a moment the Princess was too astonished to speak.

Then, as he waited, she flung her arms around him.

"Oh, Holden, Holden, how can you think of anything quite so wonderful?"

The Prince held her tightly against him.

"I knew," he said, "that I could not damage your reputation, my lovely one, and it would have been impossible for me to be alone with you for so long without making you mine."

His voice deepened as he went on,

"I want you and God knows, I have waited long enough! Now I am making sure that whatever happens in the future, nothing shall ever separate us."

"Oh, Holden, it is what I want too," the Princess cried. "But I never thought of our being married at sea."

"If our plot remains undiscovered," the Prince said, "we can be married again with all the Pomp and Ceremony which you, like all women, will love. But this, our secret marriage, will be absolutely binding."

He paused before he went on in a different voice,

"If the worst comes to the worst, and the Queen discovers what has happened, there will be nothing by the Laws of England, or by the Laws of my country, that she can do about it."

"That is what I want, that is exactly what I want," the Princess murmured.

If the Prince had wanted to say anything more, it would have been impossible.

She pulled his head down to hers and pressed her lips against his.

She kissed him with a happiness that seemed to light the whole cabin with their love.

*

On board *H.M.S. Heroic* Avila took off her black bonnet and tidied her hair in the cabin mirror.

Feeling a little nervous, but at the same time excited, she went into the cabin next door.

The Greek Ambassador and Lord Cardiff were there and they rose to their feet when she entered.

They were both, she saw, drinking a glass of sherry.

As she asked them to sit down again, the Ambassador began to pay her compliments.

He was speaking in his own language and was delighted when she replied with a fluency of Greek that he had not expected.

It was only after they had been chatting for some time that Avila realised that they were being rude to Lord Cardiff.

"I do apologise, my Lord," she said in English, "but I need to polish up my Greek before we reach Athens so that I do not miss anything that is said to me. Just as I have no wish to miss anything I can see."

Lord Cardiff laughed.

"I am afraid my Greek, ma'am, which I learnt at my school is not, shall we say, very conversational. However, I can usually manage to obtain what I want in restaurants and in shops."

"That is a step in the right direction," Avila smiled. "You will understand how exciting it will be for me to be in the country that I half-belong to for the first time since I was very small and to hear all the people speak a language which is not often heard in England."

"When we return," the Ambassador said, "I shall make certain that Your Royal Highness is notified of everything that takes place at the Embassy. I realise now that we have been very remiss in not asking you to attend when we have organised exhibitions of Greek dancing and Greek Lecturers who talk about the ancient history of Greece and its amazing ruins."

"I would love that!" Avila replied enthusiastically.

Then she remembered that it would be Princess Marigold, not she, who would be invited to attend these events.

She talked a great deal to the Ambassador about the Temples that were still standing in Delphi and the Parthenon in Athens. They spoke about the many beautiful relics that could be found on the many and different Greek islands.

"You certainly know much more about Greece, ma'am, than I might have expected," he said that night over dinner.

"And I never expected to see what I have only read about in books," Avila replied.

"So you don't remember much about the country before your father and mother came to England?" the Ambassador then asked her.

With a little throb of fear in her heart, Avila realised that she had made a mistake and it was something she must not do again.

She then tried desperately to recall just what she had been told about Princess Marigold's early life.

"I am afraid," she said after a pause, "I actually remember very little about it. I was only four years old at the time, but I can recall the garden where I played and the delightful room, which I think must have been my Nursery."

"If only you had been a little older," the Ambassador sighed. "But never mind we can make up for it now and I know, because you have Greek blood in your veins, you will find everywhere you look that there is something that pulls at your heart, and at the same time invigorates your mind."

It was something that had never been said to Avila before and it made her feel even more excited than she was already.

She would see Greece and feel the Light which her mother had told her had eventually enveloped the world.

It was a sublime Light that not only dazzled the eyes, but had made the Greeks give the civilised world the power to think, to plan and to create.

That night, when she went to bed in her cabin, Avila prayed,

'Thank You God, for letting me come on this wonderful voyage of discovery. Forgive me for deceiving my Papa and let me find in Greece the answer to the many questions about life that have always intrigued and puzzled me.'

It was a very sincere prayer.

Then she snuggled down against her soft pillows and she felt the ship's engines turning beneath her.

She was thinking how incredibly fortunate she was.

A new world was opening out before her, a world that was so much a part of her blood, and she knew as well that it was also part of her heart and her soul.

'Greece, the Gateway of the Mind'.

The Light which had been first lit by the God of Light himself.

Apollo!

CHAPTER FOUR

As the Battleship steamed on through the Mediterranean, Avila knew that she had never enjoyed herself so much in her entire life.

Ever since they had left Tilbury, Lady Bedstone had remained in her cabin.

She had refused to move until they had passed through the Bay of Biscay and this meant that Avila had the two elderly gentlemen to herself.

They complimented and praised her and talked to her ceaselessly about all the things that she found interesting about Ancient Greece and Modern Greece.

At first it seemed strange to be addressed as 'Your Royal Highness' or 'ma'am', but she soon grew used to it.

Equally she could not help wishing that her mother was with her and she knew just how much she would have enjoyed listening to the Greek Ambassador and his many recollections.

Avila learnt stories about Greece that she had never known about and was wildly excited when they eventually reached Athens.

H.M.S. Heroic steamed into the Port at exactly the expected time of arrival, which was midday.

The quay that they docked at was decorated with a profusion of Greek flags and Union Jacks intwined.

As Avila looked down at the large gathering crowd, the Ambassador told her,

"I can see the Prime Minister, so be prepared for a lengthy welcome."

"At last I am really in Greece!" Avila enthused in a rapt tone.

In the distance she could see the Sacred Rock of the Acropolis with the Parthenon on the top of it.

Because it was all so thrilling, she wanted to clap her hands and cheer.

Then she became aware that seeing her on deck the people on the quay were waving and shouting out 'welcome' in Greek.

The Ambassador rather stiffly led her down the gangway.

As he had warned her, the Prime Minister was there to greet her together with a number of other senior Statesmen.

Avila was given a large bouquet of flowers by a pretty small girl with long hair wearing a colourful dress.

There were three speeches of welcome, each one longer than the last.

.Avila was delighted that she was able to understand every word they said to her, but she thought that it was all too much talk even though Great Britain was their very strong ally.

Then in an open carriage she was driven to the British Embassy where she was to stay.

The Ambassador had already explained that it had been first thought that she would not be staying at The Royal Palace since the King was away visiting his relations in Denmark.

It was one thing, Avila thought, to deceive the Ambassador and the Prime Minister that she was a 'Royal Highness'.

It was quite another to deceive a King!

She was well aware, because her mother had told her, of the difficulties there had been in Greece after they had deposed King Otto.

At last they had now found the King they required.

There had been a number of different candidates.

Finally the search had ended with William, the seventeen-year-old second son of the heir to the Throne of Denmark.

The Treaty of Accession had been signed in London all of twenty-three years ago by the representatives of Great Britain, France, Austria, Prussia and Russia.

The new King took the title of 'George I of the Hellenes'.

It had been easy for him to sign a protocol to become their King, but difficult to win the acceptance of the many Principalities and leading Greek families.

They all had their spheres of influence and wished to keep the power that they had held over the centuries.

Avila was glad that she did not have to listen to the many problems and squabbles which had ensued.

The British Embassy was a large and delightful building set in a large garden filled with exotic flowers.

The British Ambassador to Greece welcomed her with yet another speech, but not such a long one. He explained that his wife was unfortunately abroad, which Avila thought was a relief.

A woman, she felt, was far more likely than a man to notice if she did or said anything wrong or misleading.

Avila was therefore chaperoned by Lady Bedstone, who made a tremendous effort to be charming to everyone who spoke to her and even tried to speak a few words of Greek herself.

The funeral they soon learned was to take place the next day.

Avila wondered if she could say that there were a number of sights that she would like to see that afternoon.

It was then that the Greek Ambassador said to her,

"I think I should explain to Your Royal Highness that the deceased Prince Eumenus had no sons. His nephew, His Royal Highness Prince Darius of Kanidos, will therefore be looking after you and I am only surprised that he is not here already."

"His Royal Highness did say," a member of his staff who had joined them interposed, "that he had to see the Priests about the Funeral Service and so might be a little late."

"Oh, yes, of course," the Ambassador agreed, "I had forgotten."

Even as he spoke a servant announced,

"His Royal Highness Prince Darius of Kanidos."

Avila turned to see the Prince coming into the room.

He was certainly very good-looking.

In fact, as he advanced towards her, she could not help thinking that he might have been the model for a statue of Apollo.

He had perfectly chiselled features and her mother had told Avila that these were most characteristic of the aristocratic Greeks. He also had the lithe physique of an athlete and his dark eyes somehow resembled her own.

As he came nearer, Avila realised that he was looking at her searchingly as well as with an expression of surprise.

"Let me please present, Your Royal Highness," the British Ambassador was now saying, "His Royal Highness Prince Darius of Kanidos, who will be very delighted to show you all the famous sights of Athens."

Avila put out her hand.

When the Prince took it, she felt strange vibrations coming from his fingers.

It made her think that he was even more like a God than he had at first appeared.

She remembered that, when Apollo flew across the sky, flashing with a million points of Light and healing everyone he touched, he germinated the seeds of life and defied the Powers of Darkness.

She did not know why that particular description had suddenly come into her mind.

But it came to her again even more vividly as the Prince held her hand in his.

Almost as if he was speaking to himself, he sighed,

"You are even more beautiful than I expected you to be!"

Avila blushed and he added,

"I was told to show you the beauties of Athens, but now I want Athens to see you!"

What he said so charmingly sounded different in Greek from how it would have sounded in English.

Avila was thinking that no one had ever said anything so wonderful to her before.

When they went into luncheon, the Prince was seated on her right.

He then asked her what she wanted particularly to see while she was staying in Greece.

"Everything!" she almost demanded. "I cannot believe that I am really here as I have read about Greece and talked about it, but thought I would never actually be able to see it as I can now."

There was no mistaking the enthusiasm and excitement in her voice.

The Prince then suggested quietly,

"I believe you are here for only a short time, but I promise I will not allow you to waste a minute. This afternoon I will take you first to the Parthenon."

Avila gave a little cry of delight.

"I saw it! I could see it from the ship as we came into Port. It looked exactly as I always believed it would."

"We will go there as soon as we have finished luncheon," the Prince said, "but you must remember that nobody hurries in Athens."

He smiled before he added,

"The women walk slowly and gracefully and the *cafés* are full of men gossiping."

Avila laughed.

"But I shall have to hurry, otherwise, how else am I to see everything in Greece before the Battleship carries me back to England?"

"I have a distinct feeling that there are to be more speeches to listen to when luncheon is finished, but with your permission I will suggest that they are kept until after dinner tonight when it will be too dark to show you the beauty of Athens."

"Oh, yes, please arrange it," Avila pleaded.

Because she was so excited she grudged the time they took to eat the delicious food they were offered.

As the Prince had suggested, he asked the Ambassador that there should be no speeches until this evening,

"Her Royal Highness wishes to see the whole of Greece in a few days," he said, "but, as that is impossible, I have to show her at least the most beautiful places before she returns to her own country."

There was a murmur of agreement at this proposal.

Finally, even sooner than Avila might have anticipated, they had left the Embassy and were driving in an open carriage along the road that led to the Acropolis.

Lady Bedstone had to go with them.

Avila however, told her in a whisper that she was to stay in the carriage and not to try to walk up to the Parthenon on the summit of the Acropolis.

Lady Bedstone was only too delighted to stay where she was and, as she had enjoyed the luncheon, Avila was certain that, if she had the opportunity, she would soon drop off to sleep.

The horses climbed as far as they could up to the great entrance portal of the Acropolis.

Then the Prince sprang out of the carriage and held out his hand to Avila.

Again she felt that strange and unusual vibration.

It seemed in some odd way that she did not understand, to link her with him.

The Parthenon itself was even grander and more impressive than she had ever imagined. It rose above the purple rock like a great ship with all its sails flying.

"That is what I have always thought," the Prince told her quietly.

She turned to stare at him.

"You are reading my thoughts."

"I realised at luncheon that it was what I could do," the Prince said. "I cannot explain it, but why should we want to?"

There was something in the way he looked at Avila that made her feel a little confused.

Because she was beginning to feel shy, she began to ask him a multitude of questions.

He told her how the marble of the Parthenon had been painted with different colours of blue, scarlet and gold.

"Today however," he said quietly, "we see it as the Greeks saw it perhaps around 440 B.C. shortly before it was finished."

They wandered amongst its many columns and the Prince quoted the words of Pericles.

He had claimed that the Parthenon was built so '*the heart may be warmed and the eye delighted for ever*'.

"That is exactly what has happened," Avila said. "One cannot help just looking at it and being delighted. At the same time it makes me feel small and unimportant."

"That is something you could never be," the Prince smiled at her.

He next took her to the Erechtheion, the ancient Temple dedicated to the glory of the Goddess Athena. The six figures had been sculpted in the form of beautiful maidens in a rare but lovely form of architecture.

The Prince then told her that columns sculpted in this way were known as Karyatids. The word meant '*maidens of the little country town of Karyar*'.

They were widely noted for performing ritual dances in which they sometimes posed in this attitude.

Avila stood looking at them and thinking how beautiful and at the same time mysterious they were. She felt that the Erechtheion had a special feeling of sanctity about it.

Then she became aware that Prince Darius was gazing at her.

As if the Prince was again reading her thoughts, he said,

"The sacred robe of Athene was preserved here. It was here too that the golden lamp was never allowed to go out."

"I wish I could have seen Athene!" Avila remarked.

"I am seeing her!" the Prince answered.

She looked at him in some surprise.

Then, when she realised what he had meant, she blushed.

"This is the right place for you," he said softly. "While the Parthenon is masculine, the Erechtheion is wholly feminine. I feel certain that you have been here before and, as Athene belonged to the Light, so do you."

Avila drew in her breath.

She could hardly believe that anyone was actually saying these things to her that she had thought of only in her dreams.

From what she had read about the Gods and Goddesses she had imagined that she herself was one of them.

She knew that nothing in the world could be more complimentary than that the Prince should think of her in the same breath as Athene.

Then very softly he went on,

"Athene meant so much to the Ancient Greeks and she was worshipped by them under so many conflicting aspects."

His voice deepened as he continued,

"There was 'Athene the Warrior', shaking her tall spear, 'Athene the Companion' and 'Athene of the Household'. She was Goddess of all things fair and she was as well 'Athene the Virgin', who was determined to protect the virginity of her beloved City."

"That is so – beautiful – the way you say it," Avila murmured.

There was a little pause before the Prince replied,

"There was also 'Athene the Goddess of Love'. I always think of these maidens whom we have just been admiring as if they were Priestesses of Athene as the Goddess of Love."

He looked down at Avila and then added,

"Now I know exactly why I have always been drawn to the Erechtheion more than to the Parthenon itself."

Avila felt that if he said anything more, it might spoil the wonder of what had already been spoken.

She therefore started to walk down towards the carriage.

The Prince moved beside her without protest. She knew that it was because once again he had been reading her thoughts.

'How is it possible,' she asked herself now, 'that he can know what I am thinking?'

Yet she was aware that they were speaking without having to use words.

It was so strange and so unexpected that she began to feel a little frightened.

Then, as they neared the carriage, the Prince said softly,

"Don't be afraid. Because you are Greek you will hear things that the other people don't hear and see things that other people do not see. They are all part of the wonder and glory of this marvellous land which gives a Divine radiance to those who belong to it."

They then arrived back at the carriage and Lady Bedstone, who had been fast asleep on the cushions, woke up.

"I hope you have enjoyed yourselves," she remarked sleepily.

It was then that Avila felt that she had been brought back to reality from another world.

*

They dined early.

The British Ambassador had invited a large party to meet, as they supposed, Her Royal Highness the Princess Marigold.

There were a number of pleasant young Greek men, but somehow they did not compare with Prince Darius.

Even when he was at the other end of the room talking to a group of guests, Avila was acutely aware of him.

As he was so handsome, she found it impossible not to keep thinking of him as the God Apollo.

She could also feel him vibrating towards her, so that it was very difficult to follow the conversation of anyone who was talking to her.

At one moment during the evening she went to the window.

She wanted to view the lights that were gleaming in every window within sight and the stars were twinkling above the Parthenon.

Her mother had told her how the Greeks loved light and they never tired of describing the appearance of it.

"They like the glitter of stones and sand washed by the sea," Mrs. Grandell said, "of fish churning in the nets and they chose for the site of the Temple to Apollo twin cliffs which are called 'The Shining Ones'."

'I would love to go and visit Delphi,' Avila thought now, but she was sure that it was too far away.

If she went, she just knew that she would want to see Delphi with Prince Darius walking beside her.

Even as she thought of him she was aware that he had joined her at the window.

"No other people but the Greeks," he said quietly, "leave so many lights burning at night. Light is their protection against the evil of darkness."

"I have heard that," Avila murmured.

She looked up at him and he went on,

"The Ancient Greeks well understood the depth of darkness in the human soul and they believed that at night their souls was at the mercy of their evil imaginings."

"I suppose too they were very superstitious," Avila commented.

"They refused to allow any superstition to ride roughshod over them," the Prince replied, "and they believed, as I do, that the Light of the mind can put an end to the darkness of the soul."

Avila stared at him.

She was thinking that this was a very strange conversation to be having with a young man.

Yet it was the sort of subject that she had talked about with her mother and sometimes in a rather different way with her father.

"You have come to see Greece," the Prince went on, "but in fact you already know the answers to the things which have puzzled your mind and which you questioned before you came here."

"How do you know that?" Avila asked.

"Because only a Greek can understand Greece and I knew this afternoon, as I know now, there is really nothing that I need explain to you. For the answer is there already in your heart and, of course, your soul."

As he finished speaking, their eyes met.

And then suddenly much to her surprise, he turned without another word and walked away from her.

He left the room and for a moment she could not believe that he had actually gone.

He did not return and she felt that the room seemed empty and barren without him.

Suddenly the light had disappeared and there was a darkness that she could not explain.

An hour later she went up to bed.

She was thinking that despite all the discussions with her mother and the books she had read, she had come nearer to understanding Greece in these last few hours than she ever had before.

She owed it, she knew, to Prince Darius who had suddenly left her as if he was indeed Apollo himself.

'Perhaps he was already 'driving his chariot across the sky' to another part of the world,' she mused.

'I will I see him again tomorrow,' Avila told herself before she went to sleep.

*

Prince Holden's yacht was anchored in a little bay along the French coast.

The Marriage had taken place as soon as the yacht was in the English Channel.

Princess Marigold had worn the white gown, the wreath of orchids on her head and she carried a bouquet.

She had gone into the Saloon where Captain Bruce was waiting to perform the Marriage Ceremony. He was looking very smart in his uniform and was proudly wearing his medals.

Prince Holden was already there waiting for her, wearing, as was indeed correct on the Continent, evening dress.

There were several Orders sparkling with diamonds pinned to the breast of his cut-away coat and a star on a red ribbon showed from under his cravat.

Taking Princess Marigold's hand, he stood with her before the Captain, who was holding a Prayer Book in his right hand.

Then he solemnly began the Marriage Service.

He married them according to the rights that were given to every ship's Captain. It had been made the Law that a Captain could marry legally at sea any of those travelling in the ship that he commanded.

To Princess Marigold, the words were as moving as if her Wedding was taking place in St. Paul's Cathedral.

When finally Captain Bruce had finished the Service and pronounced them to be man and wife, she felt as if there were angels singing in chorus overhead.

The Captain gave them his good wishes, smiled at them and left them alone together.

It was then that Princess Marigold turned towards Prince Holden and enthused,

"We are married! We are really married and now I am your wife!"

"Do you suppose, my darling, that I am not aware of that?" he asked her.

He put his arms around her and then looked down at her with a serious expression in his eyes.

"You are mine, my wife, and no one can take you from me. At the same time I swear to you before God that I will do everything in my power to make you happy and make sure that you never regret giving yourself to me."

"It is the most – wonderful thing that – ever happened to me," Princess Marigold said, "and the reason why I did not – accept anyone else was that I knew that somewhere in the world there was *you* and – I belonged to you."

"Perhaps in very many lives before this," the Prince said. "Personally, I am completely and utterly content that we are now together whatever the difficulties may be in the future."

"There will be none," Princess Marigold declared. "I feel that the Gods are with us, the Gods of Greece, in whom my father so believed, and who have guarded me and brought you into – my life."

"That is just what I believe too," the Prince said. "My darling, I am the luckiest and most fortunate man in the whole wide world."

He pulled her against him and kissed her until the Saloon swung round them.

Then he raised his head and said,

"We are married, my precious Marigold, and because I want to make sure of it, let's now go below."

"We will," the Princess agreed, "and do you realise my wonderful husband – that nobody can interrupt us? There are no Equerries no *aides-de-camp* outside the door and no Ladies-in-Waiting making certain that I am not alone with you."

She laughed and added,

"And for the moment no disagreeable Queen determined to separate us."

Prince Holden kissed her forehead.

"Not even Queen Victoria can do that now and, as you agreed, my beautiful wife, let's go where we will not be interrupted by anyone."

They went below.

The sunshine was streaming in through the portholes of the Master cabin.

It dazzled Princess Marigold's eyes and glinted strongly on her golden hair.

The Prince locked the door of the cabin.

Then, as they looked at each other lovingly, they both realised just how fundamentally they had revolted against protocol.

In fact against everything that they had been brought up to revere and observe.

They had started a revolution all of their own and now, for the moment at any rate, they were triumphantly free.

The Princess threw out her arms.

As the Prince held her against him, they were both aware that they had fought a battle against what had seemed overwhelming odds and had emerged victorious.

*

A long time later Princess Marigold stirred against her husband's shoulder.

"My precious, my darling," he sighed. "I have not hurt or frightened you?"

"Why did you not – tell me before that love was so wonderful?" the Princess whispered. "I felt as if it – carried me up to the sky – and I touched star after star."

"That is what I wanted you to feel, my darling."

There had been a number of women in his life. But he had never known anyone who could evoke in him the rapture that he felt with the Princess.

He knew that it was because they felt for each other the real love that all men seek but very seldom find.

It was the love of the mind as well as the body and the soul as well as the heart.

He had known from the moment that he first saw the Princess that she was everything he desired and needed as his wife.

Yet she was important.

He was only a very minor Royal compared to her and he had thought that it would be impossible ever to claim her for his own.

Now, by the mercy of God and a great deal of scheming on his part, they had managed to escape from the prison of convention into a delightful world of their own.

He could hardly believe it to be possible.

It had persisted in his thoughts by day and by night that they must be together.

Not only for the two weeks of what he knew would be a blissful honeymoon but for the rest of their lives together.

He was certain that there would be difficulties about it and so without doubt they would both suffer for the deception that they had perpetrated when it was discovered.

He told himself, however, it would be well worth it for the happiness they wcrc feeling now. It was the sublime happiness that he had been desperately afraid would elude him for ever.

"Are you – thinking about – me?" the Princess asked him in a soft little voice.

"How could I think of anything else?" the Prince asked. "Actually I was thanking God that we have been so fortunate as to get away without being stopped, to be married without being prevented from doing so and to know that, hard though the future may be, this moment is ours."

He kissed her eyes as he spoke.

Then, because she lifted her mouth to his, he kissed her lips.

He felt the fire of love moving within them both.

He told himself that anything that happened in the future was unimportant beside what was happening to them now at this very moment.

Then the flames that were leaping higher and higher encompassed them both.

CHAPTER FIVE

The funeral was very impressive in the small but charming early Byzantine Kapnikarea Church.

Built in the tenth century in the shape of a cross, its cupola was supported by four long columns.

Avila found herself responding to the beauty of the music, the fragrance of the incense and the seven silver lights hanging in front of the screen behind which lay the sanctuary.

The coffin had mounds of flowers piled around it.

Prince Darius had told Avila that anyone of any importance in Athens would be present at the funeral.

She was very glad that she had her black bonnet with its long veil over her face.

She could look at the people around her without them being able to see her at all closely.

She had never heard a choir singing in Greek before and she thought that the beauty of the words matched the music.

When finally the Funeral Service came to an end, everyone filed past the coffin and bent over to kiss the dead man's cheek.

Prince Darius escorted Avila out of the Church first before anyone else had left.

She had learnt that King George was definitely not coming to the funeral as he was still in Denmark with his family.

She thought that Prince Darius and the Officials were rather relieved that there was not even more protocol for them to attend to.

She walked out into the sunshine in silence with Prince Darius thinking how exceedingly smart she looked.

Lady Bedstone, who had sat at the back of the Church at her own request, was standing by the closed carriage that was waiting outside when Avila reached it.

As Prince Darius handed her into it, he told her in a low voice,

"I shall be picking you up after the luncheon. The Ambassador will tell you what I have planned."

She smiled at him through her veil and then the carriage drove away.

Now when they were alone, Avila lifted her veil and threw it back over her bonnet.

"Have you heard what is being planned for this afternoon?" she enquired.

"His Excellency did say that you were going somewhere," Lady Bedstone said vaguely. "I am afraid that I did not hear where it was."

They drove on in silence to the British Embassy.

Prince Darius had told her yesterday that an official luncheon was being given for the relatives and close friends of the deceased, which he must attend.

He thought that she would find it all rather boring, so instead she was to have luncheon in the Embassy.

She kept wondering now where he would take her after luncheon.

There was so much she wanted to see, but she realised despondently that there was only one full day left before they must return to England.

Lord Cardiff had made this very clear when he had said,

"I know, ma'am, that you will understand that I have so many duties in England to cope with that I cannot afford to be away longer from home than is absolutely necessary."

It was with difficulty that Avila had not replied that she had plenty of time on her hands as far as Greece was concerned. She would have liked to stay here for weeks more to see everything that there was to be seen.

Now, as they reached the British Embassy and she saw the Union Flag flying outside in the breeze, she knew that she wanted to stay not only to see more of Greece but also to stay longer with Prince Darius.

She just could not imagine that there could be anything more fascinating than to hear him telling her about the Gods and Goddesses of Ancient Greece and explaining to her as he had yesterday the secrets of the Parthenon and the Erechtheion.

'I have one more day,' she said to herself as the sentries saluted her when she went into the Embassy.

It was quite a small party at luncheon to Avila's relief.

The Ambassador talked most of the time with Lord Cardiff about the current situation in the Balkans.

Avila could not help thinking that she had never known an hour pass more slowly.

When luncheon was ended and she went into the drawing room with Lady Bedstone, she thought despairingly that time was being wasted when she might be out sightseeing.

Then the British Ambassador came into the room rather hurriedly.

"I am so sorry, Your Royal Highness," he said apologetically, "I quite forgot what Prince Darius asked me to tell you."

For one moment Avila thought the Prince was not coming to see her after all and she felt her heart drop.

"As he is most anxious for you to see his house," the Ambassador added, "and also, I understand, one of the islands tomorrow, he has now suggested that you and Lady Bedstone should stay the night with him."

Avila gave a little murmur of excitement as the Ambassador went on,

"I am sure you will be impressed with Kanidos, which is a very beautiful part of Greece. The Prince's house is not very far away from here along the coast road leading South to Cape Sounion."

He paused a moment and then resumed,

"This, as I am sure you know, is the most southerly point of Attica, the comparatively small area of which in Classical times Athens was the Capital."

"I should love to see the Prince's house," Avila commented, trying hard not to sound too pleased.

"It is certainly very impressive," the Ambassador replied, "and I expect your maid will have already packed your clothes."

"What time are we leaving?" Avila asked him.

"The Prince will be calling for you," the Ambassador answered, "as soon as his luncheon is finished. These wakes, as they call them in Scotland, usually go on for hours and hours."

He smiled at her before continuing,

"But I am sure that the Prince will be able to excuse himself. I should think he will be here very soon."

To Avila this was splendid news.

She went straight upstairs to her room to find, as the Ambassador had told her, that her Greek maid had already packed her trunk.

She did, however, change out of the elaborate and rather thick dress she had worn to the funeral into something lighter as it was becoming much warmer.

Because the sun was shining she was only sorry that she could not wear one of the pretty muslin gowns that she wore at home.

She then looked at herself in the mirror somewhat despairingly.

She was not aware that black in fact accentuated the transparency of her skin and made her hair appear even more golden than usual.

'Do I really have to wear this bonnet with its crêpe veil?' she asked herself.

She knew the answer at once, 'mourning is mourning', especially when it had anything to do with Her Majesty Queen Victoria.

Avila had just finished getting ready when a servant announced that His Royal Highness was downstairs.

It was with difficulty that she managed to walk down slowly with what she hoped was dignity.

The Prince was waiting for her in the drawing room and she could see at once that he had changed from the conventional clothes that he had worn in the morning.

"I have only just been told by His Excellency – that we are to stay – with you tonight," Avila managed to stammer and trying extra hard not to sound too enthusiastic. It is a lovely surprise that I am very much looking forward to."

"Not as much as I am," the Prince answered. "The carriages are outside."

, "The carriages?" Avila questioned.

"Lady Bedstone told me that she much preferred travelling in a closed carriage, while I thought that you would like to be able to see the wonderful countryside we shall be passing through."

"Of course I would," Avila exclaimed.

She spoke so fervently that she thought that perhaps she was being indiscreet.

There was, she suspected, a twinkle in the Prince's eyes.

However, as she was in a hurry to get away, they went straight out to where the carriages were waiting.

She found that the Prince had a smart grand chaise that he would be driving her in. And the sides of the chaise were emblazoned with his Royal Coat-of-Arms.

It was not unlike the one that Prince Holden drove, but slightly more elaborate.

It was also, Avila soon discovered, very comfortable and luxurious.

The Prince helped her in and the Ambassador waved them goodbye.

The chaise was drawn by two chestnut horses that were perfectly matched and she knew that they were very well-bred,

They drew them out of Athens very quickly.

To begin with they travelled almost in silence and, when there was no longer any traffic and the country in all its loveliness was on either side of them, Avila began,

"I was wondering this morning what you had planned for me. I had no idea that it would be as exciting as this."

"That is what I want you to feel," the Prince said. "I know how very little time we have."

He emphasised the word '*we*'.

Avila then replied,

"I feel perhaps that I should not have taken you away from your uncle's funeral."

"I have left a number of relatives to act as hosts to the other mourners," the Prince said. "I have so much to show you in so short a time that we must not miss a second of it."

"That is what I have been thinking," Avila nodded.

She was aware that the Prince was a very good driver and he had complete control over his two horses.

She had never seen anything so lovely as when a little later they had the sea on one side of them and the land green with the leaves of Spring on the other.

There were tall mountains in the far distance and there seemed to be very few inhabitants about.

Avila thought that they were all alone in a magical world which belonged to the Gods of Greece.

"Another time," the Prince said, "I will take you to Delphi. But tomorrow I have another rather special place to show you, which I feel you will appreciate because you are Greek and because to Greeks it is the most sacred place in the world."

Avila looked at him in surprise wondering what he meant as then he added,

"I shall keep it a secret until tomorrow. Today I want you to concentrate on me. We are now in my territory, which my family has reigned over for many generations."

It was certainly exceedingly beautiful with its lines of olive trees and distant mountains.

It was nearly two hours before Avila saw a little ahead of them a large building that was gleaming white in the sunshine.

For a moment she thought that it must be a Temple to one of the many Gods.

Then, as the Prince drove nearer towards the large building she asked him,

"Is this your house?"

"Yes it is," he replied, "and you will find it, in every way, very Greek."

"It looks like a Palace," Avila said as they drew nearer and she saw how huge it was.

"It was originally built as one," the Prince explained. "We were Kings in Medieval times when Greece consisted of a number of small Kingdoms, which were usually at war with one another."

"And now?" Avila asked.

"We would hope, if the Russians will leave us alone, to remain happily and prosperously united under our one King."

"I am sure that your Gods will help you to obtain your heart's desire," Avila murmured.

"That is exactly what I am hoping they will do for me," the Prince said quickly.

There was a meaning in his voice that she could not misunderstand.

She now blushed a little and deliberately looked ahead of her, hoping that he would not notice.

"You are very lovely," the Prince was saying to her softly. "But I am going to talk about that tomorrow!"

Avila longed to know why he had to wait until tomorrow.

But she recognised that it was a question that she could not ask him.

They were now drawing nearer and nearer to the beautiful house that lay just ahead of them and with its Ionic columns and exquisite proportions it looked even more like a Temple to the Gods than when she had first seen it.

The Prince drew his horses to a standstill with a flourish.

Servants came tumbling out of the front door of the house to greet them.

And Lady Bedstone was not far behind.

By the time Avila had taken off her bonnet and tidied her hair, her Lady-in-Waiting and her lady's maid had come upstairs.

"I hope the journey was not too tiring for you," Avila addressed Lady Bedstone.

"To be honest, ma'am," Lady Bedstone replied, "I slept most of the way. The carriage was so comfortable that it really lulled me into a deep sleep."

She yawned before she asked,

"I hope Your Royal Highness will understand that now we have arrived I would like to rest. Then I will not be too tired to come down to dinner."

"Yes, of course," Avila agreed. "As soon as you are unpacked, I should then get into bed. I am sure if you would like a cup of tea someone will bring it to you."

She saw the relief on the old lady's face and hurried downstairs.

The Prince was alone in one of the most beautiful rooms that she had ever seen.

The rooms at Windsor Castle were filled with a clutter of small tables, *objets d'art* and endless photographs.

The lovely drawing room contained all the most essential furniture and three outstanding pictures. It was in fact a picture or even a poem in itself.

"This is the loveliest room I have ever seen," Avila exclaimed.

"That is what I hoped you would think," the Prince answered. "And it is, as I expected, a frame for you and your beauty."

"That is the nicest compliment I have ever had," Avila smiled.

"I can think of a number of others," the Prince replied. "As I have supplied you with an English tea, I shall be disappointed if you don't enjoy it."

At his suggestion she poured out two cups of tea for them both.

He took the cup from her, but he did not drink it.

Instead he sat down in a nearby chair looking at her in a way which made her feel shy.

"How can you be anything at the moment," the Prince asked, "but 'Athene, the Goddess of the Household'?"

Avila laughed.

You are well aware," she answered, " that Athene had dark hair and, so I suspect, did all the other Goddesses. So I don't really fit in."

"'*Athene was the Goddess of all things fair*'," the Prince then quoted, "and, as she like Apollo, was enveloped with Light, I imagine your golden hair would have been appropriate for those who wanted to sculpt her."

"I doubt it," Avila replied, "and I suppose we shall never know the truth of what exactly they did look like."

The Prince threw up his hands.

"A million or more statues have been made of Athene! But, of course, in a way you are right. It is only when I can see her living and breathing that I am now aware of how beautiful she is."

Avila understood what he was implying.

Somehow, because they were speaking Greek, his compliments were not as embarrassing as they would have been in English.

"You said you had brought me here to see your house," she said quickly, "Now tell me exactly when it was built and who designed it so perfectly that it appears to be a Temple?"

The Prince answered her questions.

Then when they had finished their tea, he took her on a tour round the house.

He showed her the many rooms which were exquisitely furnished and the sunken bath which was still intact.

He claimed that he intended to use it when it had been completely restored to its former beauty.

Then, when the sun was sinking in the sky. they went out into the garden.

In the distance Avila could see the deep blue of the sea and the vague outline of several Islands.

"You must tell me about these Islands," she suggested.

"That is something I shall be doing tomorrow," the Prince replied.

"It is something you have been saying all day and I am wondering why tomorrow will be any different from today."

"That is a question I can only answer tomorrow," he responded with a smile.

She laughed.

"Now you are being mysterious. I am not sure if it is a game you are playing to amuse yourself or whether there really is something mysterious about what we shall do tomorrow."

"I am afraid you will just have to wait and see," the Prince answered enigmatically.

Avila laughed again.

"I suppose it is because we are in Greece. We seem to be talking in a strange manner, as if we were imitating the Sages and all those great men who lived and wrote in Athens."

"How could we do better?" .the Prince answered. "As Sophocles said, '*Many marvels there are, but none so marvellous as man*'."

"My mother has often quoted it to me," Avila said, "but I thought it was extremely unfair and typically male that he did not mention women."

The Prince chuckled.

"I think that he was well aware that sooner or later women would push themselves to the front and affirm that they were more marvellous than men!"

He paused for a moment for reflection and then went on,

"At the same time Sophocles and every other deep thinker worshipped Athene as well as the other Goddesses of Mount Olympus."

"It is an odd thing," Avila said, "that ever since I have been in Greece I have realised that it is difficult to have a conversation that the ancient Gods and Goddesses are not included in."

"I thought you would understand that they are included because you are aware, as I am, that they are still here amongst us."

Avila looked at him.

"Do you really believe that? Do you think they are on Mount Olympus at this moment, laughing at us?"

"I don't know whether it is Olympus or anywhere else in Greece," the Prince said. "But I am very sure as you are, if you will allow yourself to admit it, that the Gods and Goddesses are still alive and still leading us in their own way to the full understanding of life which they possess."

The way he spoke was very moving and Avila clasped her hands together.

"You make everything I find so difficult sound so very simple," she said. "Yet I suppose, when I leave, it will all be difficult again."

"Must you leave?" the Prince asked.

Because it was an unexpected question, she turned to look at him.

"I have to go home, as you know, the day after tomorrow and I shall not have seen even a quarter of what I really want to see."

"I asked you quite simply," the Prince persisted, "if you must go."

Avila was about to say that she wanted to stay more than she had wanted anything in her whole life.

Then she remembered that she was not just unimportant Avila Grandell but Her Royal Highness Princess Marigold.

What was more she was secretly engaged to Prince Holden.

For a moment she could not find the right words to answer the Prince's question.

When she did not do so, he suddenly turned.

"I think it must be nearly time for us to dress for dinner. I have ordered a very special meal for you tonight that I hope you will enjoy. It may be selfish of me, but I have not invited anyone to meet you."

He spoke in rather a hard voice as if he was sweeping away the almost dreamy manner in which they had been talking.

Now they were walking back into the house and the shadows from the setting sun were growing longer.

'Perhaps he is hurt because I am not responding to him as I should be,' Avila thought to herself.

She felt a sudden pain in her heart because in some way that she could not explain he had gone away from her.

When they entered the house, he took her to the foot of the stairs.

He did not seem to notice when she looked up at him pleadingly.

"Thank you. Thank you very – much for showing me your garden beautiful – house and garden."

"I am so delighted," the Prince said, "that it pleases Your Royal Highness."

He spoke in what she felt was the conventional way a Statesman would have addressed her.

Then as she started to climb the stairs. he walked away from her.

'What have – I said? What have I done?' Avila asked herself frantically.

He had changed so suddenly and all in a second.

The caressing way he had spoken to her before had gone.

As she reached her bedroom, her maid was not there and she was alone.

She went to the window.

Looking out she could see the sea in the distance as she had seen it from the garden.

The olive trees were in blossom as were the flowers brilliantly enchanting by the house.

The sun was now sinking and yet its rays were still and the sky behind it was turning a soft crimson.

It was all breathtakingly beautiful.

But for the moment all Avila could only see was the Prince walking away from her.

'After tomorrow I shall never see him again,' she told herself

Her whole body seemed to cry out with the cruelty and unfairness of it all.

The maid came into the room and suggested that Avila should rest in her bed whilst she prepared her bath.

It was then brought into the room and, when the hot water had been carried upstairs and poured into it, it was scented with the oil of lilies.

Avila thought, as she stepped into it, of the sunken bath downstairs.

One day the Prince would bathe as his ancestors had bathed and she was sure that, when he was doing so, he would look like the statues of Apollo that her mother had shown her over many years.

She had thought from the first moment she saw him that he resembled Apollo.

Princess Marigold had provided her, among the clothes that she had brought with her, with some very pretty evening gowns.

They were, of course, black, but they had been made by someone with imagination as the lace was unlined and the tulle transparent.

When she was dressed, the gown seemed to her to be rather low in the front.

However it also left her arms and shoulders bare so she did not mind the rest of it being in black.

It had not struck her until now that Princess Marigold, if she had been here, would have brought some jewellery with her.

As her engagement to Prince Holden was a secret, the Princess had not been wearing a ring when they changed places in *The Traveller's Rest.*

Avila was quite sure that Prince Darius had no idea that Princess Marigold was secretly engaged.

At the same time to make her impersonation more convincing she felt that she should wear something round her neck.

As she looked at herself in the mirror, she knew that she wanted the Prince to admire her.

She wanted him to go on paying her the compliments which made her feel shy and were a music that she had never listened to before.

There was a knock on the door and the Greek maid went to answer it.

Avila heard a manservant saying,

"With His Royal Highness's compliments."

The maid came back to her carrying some flowers in her hand.

Looking at them Avila realised, though it seemed impossible, that the Prince had known what she would want.

What the maid held in her hand was a necklace made of small white flowers.

It was so delicately arranged and the flowers were so small that they might easily have been precious stones. Instead they had real petals and tiny leaves.

When she put it round her neck Avila saw that it was exactly what she wanted.

It made her look both correctly dressed and really beautiful.

There was a small bunch of the same flowers for the back of her head and the maid then pinned them in place.

When Avila looked in the mirror for a second time, she knew that she had never looked so lovely before.

Feeling a little self-conscious, but really excited, she went down the stairs.

When she walked into the drawing room, it was to find that the Prince was there alone.

Slowly, because she knew that he was watching her, she moved slowly towards him.

It was impossible to look into his eyes until she was actually standing in front of him and then, because he did not speak, she looked at him questioningly.

For a moment there was silence then he said very softly,

"Now I am quite sure that you are Athene."

The caressing tone was back in his voice and Avila felt her heart turn over.

Then he related,

"It is with many apologies that Lady Bedstone regrets that she is so tired that she feels sure that you will understand if she does not join us for dinner."

"I was afraid that it was rather a long journey for her," Avila managed to say.

"I am more delighted than I can put into words," the Prince pronounced, "that we can be alone."

Because she felt that she should now say something Avila replied,

"I am rather surprised that maybe the British Ambassador and certainly Lord Cardiff did not expect to be your guests."

"As a matter of fact I think that they did expect it," the Prince replied, "but I told them that unfortunately a great number of my relatives were coming to the funeral."

He saw the expression in Avila's eyes and added swiftly,

"I did not lie. I merely told them about my relatives and they assumed that they would be staying with me."

"Now you are being very evasive," Avila said. "But how did you know that you wanted us to be alone?"

"I did not know until I met you," the Prince replied. "Then when I saw you and thought that you must have stepped out of my dreams, I knew that I wanted to show you my house and talk to you alone."

"So it all happened on the spur of the moment."

"I think it was pre-ordained," the Prince answered. "We were both here perhaps when the house was first built."

Every word he said to Avila seemed to vibrate through her whole body.

She knew that she responded not only with her mind but with her heart and soul,

'He must not know what I feel for him,' Avila told herself rapidly.

Next with a tremendous effort she said lightly,

"You are making Greece too difficult for me to understand. Tell me now of your plans for the future. Surely you don't five here alone?"

"I am seldom alone," the Prince answered. "Again it was Fate or perhaps a Decree of the Gods, but I was abroad when my uncle died and I only returned to Greece three days ago."

He spoke as if in its own way it had been a certain triumph and Avila enquired,

"And what do you do when you are living here?"

"Look after my estate. I also play a part in the Government of Greece and at the moment I am deeply engaged in something which I will show you tomorrow."

Avila held up her hands in protest.

"We are not going back – tomorrow?" she questioned. "It will be impossible for me to sleep tonight in case I am missing something important from the moment the hands of the clock – pass midnight."

The Prince did not dispute her anxiety, but simply told her,

"Dinner is ready. May I have the honour, Your Royal Highness, of taking you in to enjoy it?"

He held out his arm as he spoke.

Avila put her hand on it delicately, exactly as her mother had taught her to do.

They walked down a long cool, beautifully arched passage which led to the Dining Hall.

As they did so, Avila thought that they might almost be husband and wife on their way to have dinner together in their own home.

It was just a passing thought.

But, as it swept through her mind, she knew that this was something she would always remember and think of when she returned home.

Then there would be no chance of her ever seeing Prince Darius again.

CHAPTER SIX

Avila woke in the morning with a growing feeling of excitement that today was going to be extremely significant for her. She was not quite sure why or how, but she felt certain that it would be.

She had gone to bed dreaming of Prince Darius.

She thought as she came downstairs that he looked even more handsome than he had in her dreams.

She had been told when her maid called her that Lady Bedstone was very sorry but she did not feel well enough to get out of bed this morning.

Avila had gone to see her in her bedroom and found that there was really nothing wrong with her.

The truth was that Lady Bedstone was afraid that she might have to walk some distance or perhaps climb up the side of a hill.

"I know what men are like," she grumbled, "when they are showing off something they prize. Quite frankly, ma'am, I am too old for it."

"I think you are being very sensible," Avila replied, "and I will tell you all about it when I come back."

When she was dressed, she found among Princess Marigold's black gowns the dress that she had worn when she had arrived at *The Traveller's Rest* in Tilbury.

It was thin and white. She put it on, thinking that she was unlikely to see anyone except for the Prince today and there was a small simple straw hat to go with it.

She still did not know where they were going.

Because she knew that the Prince was expecting her to ask questions, she deliberately did not show any curiosity.

'If he wants to seem mysterious,' she told herself 'then I will let him be up to the last moment.'

They drove for only a very short distance to a small bay where she saw that there was a yacht moored.

It was quite a small yacht and, as the Prince helped her out of the chaise, having handed the reins to a groom who had sat behind, he said,

"This is the yacht I use when I am visiting the Islands. I should have told you before that I have been made a Guardian of several Islands, the most outstanding being the one we are now going to."

"That is, of course, what I am all agog to hear about," Avila started to enthuse.

He was smiling as he observed,

"You have contained your curiosity very well and I do promise you that you will not be disappointed."

It was a glorious day with the sun shining brightly and the sea quiet and still.

As soon as they started to move away from the shore, Avila stood at the rail looking out over the Aegean Sea.

It was so lovely that she thought perhaps the Prince was just taking her on a tour of the nearby Islands.

Then as they moved through what seemed a transparent blue of the sea ahead, the Prince quizzed her,

"Have you not guessed where I am taking you?"

"I should be afraid to do so," Avila said. "You have been so mysterious that you would not be disappointed to find that I have guessed wrong."

"Look ahead!" the Prince urged.

She did and it seemed to her that there were a number of white Islands, all shining in the sun and somehow a little ghostly.

^Those are 'The Wheeling Ones'," the Prince told her softly. "They seem to wheel round one small Island which stands so lonely in their midst."

Avila gave a little start and then she cried,

"I know now where we are going."

"I thought you might guess," he answered. "Where else should I take Athene?"

"It is to Delos."

Now Avila felt a strange excitement sweeping over her.

She had heard about Delos all her life.

She knew that it was where Apollo had been born and to the Greeks it was the most Holy of all their precious Islands.

Because it was all so thrilling, she could not think of anything to say.

So they stood in silence until the yacht stopped in a bay where there was a small wooden quay.

It was built high enough for the gangway to be let down onto it.

"As I have been coming here so often," the Prince explained, "I found this bay. It saves me from going to the Port, which is the only place on the island where we would find any people."

He and Avila walked ashore.

Now, as they moved inland, she could see the low ground which was a mass of flowers.

Anemones in every colour flooded the meadows and she could see peeping through them just a few gleaming columns and ruins glittering in the sunshine.

It was so lovely that she could only stare at what she was seeing and it was impossible to put into words what she felt.

Prince Darius did not move.

Avila had the impression that there was a strange light glittering and shining in the sky and the air itself felt like a dancing flickering flame.

It was just so unusual and different from anything that she had ever experienced in her life.

Without thinking what she was doing, she then put out her hand and slipped it into the Prince's.

His fingers tightened on hers.

As he did so, she felt a mysterious quivering and could not understand if it was in the air above her or in her breast.

Then, as she walked on, looking at the beauty of the flowers and the distant hills, she had for a moment a very special picture in front of her.

The whole island shone white with Temples.

At the same time she was sure that she heard the beating of silver wings and the whirring of silver wheels. Always in tradition these were the outward signs that Apollo himself was present and protecting them.

How long they stood there just holding hands she had no idea.

Then she was forced to close her eyes because her feelings were too intense to bear.

The Prince then said quietly,

"The God of Light was born here and the Greeks are perfectly aware of the very strange quality of Light that illuminates this island."

"I can – feel it," Avila said in a whisper.

"As I knew you would," the Prince answered her with a shining smile on his lips.

He drew her forward and they started to walk over the anemones.

As he did so, he related,

"This is the virgin Island and no one was allowed to be born, to die or to be sick here. As you have just felt, a Divine Light covers the whole of Delos in glory."

"That is true. Really – true," Ayila said in a rapt voice. "When I read about – Delos I had no idea that

~111~

I could feel like this, exactly as – if Apollo was – still here."

"But he is!" the Prince insisted firmly. "Every time I come here I become more and more aware that the Light of the Island still comes exclusively from him."

They walked on through the anemones.

In front of them there was a small hill which the Prince told Avila was once covered with Temples. And there were the ruins of them still visible between the anemones, the ivy and the barley-grass.

Avila could see many ruins of Parian marble and she then had the strange impression that the stones were only waiting to rise again.

As she and the Prince moved amongst the ruins, she was aware of the quietness of an unexplained mystery.

They walked for quite some time and then unexpectedly she saw some olive trees.

Under them stood a table covered with a pure white cloth on which there were arranged various dishes and plates.

She looked at the Prince for an explanation and he told her,

"Here it is, our luncheon. I felt that we would not want to be waited on by servants who might interrupt our thoughts and our feelings. So we will help ourselves."

"How could you think of anything quite so delightful?" Avila asked.

"I was thinking of you," he answered.

They sat down at the table and there were the most delicious dishes to eat which only the Greeks could make.

There was a delicious golden wine to drink that Avila thought must be the nectar of the Gods.

While they were eating, the Prince told her how in later times many of the lesser Gods came here to shelter under the wings of Apollo.

"There were Temples here to Cybele, Hadad, Astarte and Isis and the Island became so sacred that few Kings, however avaricious, ever dared attack it."

"It must have been very very beautiful," Avila sighed.

"It was so beautiful, with so many treasures on it, that almost every country in the world has managed to steal what was our heritage."

His voice sharpened as he went on angrily,

"The Ottoman Turks sent expeditions to the island and then knocked down the statues of the Gods and to lop off legs, arms and heads. They transported the marble trunks and torsos to Constantinople."

"How could they do – anything so – ghastly?" Avila wanted to know.

"All men are greedy," he replied. "But I believe there are still treasures here hidden deep in the ground, which have not yet been discovered even after two thousand years of pilfering. I intend to find these for Greece and to keep them for her."

Avila looked around at the anemones and wondered if there really was anything left of the sublime glory that had been Apollo's.

They had finished their luncheon and the Prince rose and put up his hand.

"Come with me," he suggested, "and I will show you what I have found."

Avila's eyes fit up.

"Can there really," she asked him, "be anything left behind – after all these years?"

The Prince did not reply.

He was climbing up the low hill that was just behind where they had been eating.

They had reached some way up when the Prince put out his arm and they stopped.

Then, as Avila looked to the right, she saw what appeared to be a wooden door with a bar across it.

She glanced for at the Prince enquiringly and he said,

"Just before I had to go away I discovered a cave which I am sure that no one has found before."

He paused a moment and then carried on,

"I only had time to look at it briefly and, because I was afraid that people might explore it when I was away, I had, as you see, a door placed on the entrance which is locked."

He drew a key from his pocket, opened the padlock and raised the bolt.

He then pulled open the door, which was roughly made of a heavy wood.

Avila saw inside that there was a lantern on the floor and the Prince picked it up and lit it.

Then he suggested with a smile,

"Now we will go and explore."

She took the hand that he held out to her and, bending their heads because the cave was a low one, they moved forward.

A few seconds later it opened out into a much larger cave where the Prince was able to stand upright.

He lifted his lantern so that they could look round.

Avila could not see anything unusual and he said,

"I am sure that this cave was used by those who worshipped Apollo. It does not speak of murders or sacrifice but of faith and to me the promise of Light."

Avila made a little murmur. It was what she felt too and she was sure that the people who had come here worshipped Apollo with a pure and true faith.

The cave had an enchantment all of its own and she could feel it very strongly.

The Prince moved on.

They were just about to enter a further cave when suddenly there was a loud bang behind them.

They both started and turned round.

As they did so, Avila was aware that the light that had come from the open door had vanished and now there was only darkness.

Even as she was aware of it, she heard the bolt on the door being thrust into place.

Then came a hoarse ugly voice from that direction,

"Stay in there and rot! You have no right to be in a cave that belongs to the God Apollo."

The Prince moved quickly backwards to where they had come.

"You are making a mistake," he said in a commanding voice. 'I am Prince Darius and a Guardian of this Island of Delos. Open the door at once that you have just closed."

He waited and Avila held her breath.

Then suddenly there was a burst of shrill mad laughter.

"A Prince or beggar," the voice outside jeered, "you have no right to be here. Only the Gods themselves are allowed on this Island."

His Greek was coarse and Avila knew that the speaker came from the gutter.

At the same time there was an ominously mad note in his voice and in his laughter.

Now he was laughing again.

"You will rot in the darkness," he shouted. "You will die in agony as other thieves have died and the worms will eat your flesh."

"Now you listen to me – " the Prince began.

Even as he spoke the man was laughing again, it was a shrill, uncanny and unpleasant sound which seemed to rise to a sharp crescendo.

Then it faded slowly.

He was still laughing and Avila knew that he was moving down the hill that they had just climbed.

Then he must have hurried over the anemones until they could no longer hear him.

The Prince set down the lantern that he was holding in his hand and put his shoulder to the door.

Although he pushed against it with all his strength, it did not move an inch or even creak.

Suddenly Avila was frightened. Very frightened.

Without thinking of what she was doing, she threw herself against the Prince, clinging to him as she asked,

"Shall we – really stay here – and die?"

He then put his arms around her and without speaking bent his head and his lips were on hers.

He kissed her possessively and fiercely.

For a second she stiffened and then the wonder of his kiss swept over her and she felt her body melt into his.

He kissed her for a long time and she felt as if it was a part of the mystery, wonder and beauty of the Island of Delos.

Once again she could hear the beating of silver wings and the whirring of silver wheels.

It was only when the ecstasy of it was so wonderful that she felt she could no longer be alive that the Prince raised his head.

"My darling, my sweet glorious darling," he said a little unsteadily. "I have waited so long for this. Now

I know that you are mine, as you were meant to be a million years ago."

Avila was looking up at him and by the light of the lantern he could see the rapture in her eyes.

"I love you," he said softly. "Now tell me what you feel about me."

"I – love – you," Avila replied a little incoherently and hid her face against his shoulder.

Prince Darius held her very close.

"I swore a long time ago that I would never marry anyone until I found someone like Athene, who would feel as I feel when I come to Delos, that Apollo is here in the Light, as he had been ever since he was born."

He felt Avila quiver against him and then he went on,

"I knew when I first saw you that you were the one I have been seeking all my life and thought I would never find. Yet I had to make absolutely sure that I was not mistaken."

He drew in his breath before he continued,

"When we came here today and I saw and felt what you were feeling, I knew I had found the mystic love that all men seek and few are lucky enough to find."

He put his fingers under Avila's chin and turned her face up to his.

. "We shall be very happy together, my darling. How could we be anything else when Apollo has blessed us and we are both of us part of him and of Athene."

He kissed Avila again before he added,

"And now, my precious, we must find our way out of this dreadful mess."

Because he had made her forget anything but his kisses, Avila suddenly awoke to reality with a start.

They were locked in an obscure cave and no one might ever find them.

The Prince was reading her thoughts.

"Sooner or later my people will come to look for us. But it would be more dignified and certainly more pleasant if we could find our own way out of this prison now."

He released Avila as he spoke and picked up the lantern.

He walked back to where they had been when the door had been slammed shut behind them and they had just been stepping into a third cave.

As the Prince went ahead holding the lamp high, Avila could see that the ceiling here was higher than in the other caves.

But she thought depressingly that it was merely because the hill was rising outside.

It would not be possible to dig through it when they did not have a spade or anything to use but their own bare hands.

The Prince was looking round.

At the far end of the cave there was what looked like a great pile of earth that might have covered an Altar.

It rose up halfway between the floor and the ceiling.

"I think," he said after a moment's inspection, "it would be wiser to try to break our way out through the sides of the door."

Avila did not answer.

She was praying to the God she had always prayed to and to Apollo as well.

'Save us! Save us!' she murmured in her heart. 'It may be difficult or perhaps impossible for anyone to find us and we will be cold here at night and we will be hungry too.'

It all swept through her mind.

Equally she knew what her father would say and she herself believed that their only hope would come from a Power greater than mankind.

The Prince had already gone back into the second cave and she then ceased praying and looked up.

Next she was aware, now that he had taken the lantern with him, that there was a faint chink of light in the ceiling at the far end of the third cave.

She gave a cry of excitement and the Prince turned round.

"What is it, my darling?" he asked.

"Look at that! Look! I was praying and, when I opened my eyes again, I could see light."

The Prince came back into the first cave and saw where she was pointing.

There was, he could see, a very faint glimmer of light against the darkness of the third cave.

He took off his jacket and put it down on the ground beside the lantern.

Then he climbed up onto the mound of earth at the very far end of the cave and some of it crumbled as he did so.

Then, as he stood working with his fists at the roof above his head, he made a small hole and more light came streaming in.

He began pulling at the earth frantically to make the hole larger and still larger until the sun shone on his head and then on his face.

Even as he did so, Avila gave another cry.

The earth that he was standing on and which covered what she had thought might have been an Altar, was still crumbling away.

As it crumbled, it suddenly revealed something that was white and shiny.

Because she was so excited at what she was seeing, Avila ran forward.

She knelt down and brushed the soil from what the Prince's weight had just revealed.

Even as the Prince stepped down to join her, she realised at once that she was looking at an exquisitely carved statue.

It was cracked and one arm was missing, but it was quite impossible not to recognise that it was a statue of Apollo.

Prince Darius knelt down and put his arm round her.

"He has come to us when we most needed him," he declared. "I am very grateful, my darling. But even more grateful because he has given me you."

Then he was kissing her again.

Kissing her with wild and passionate kisses that were not only an expression of love.

They also expressed his utter relief that the fear of what might have happened to them had completely dissolved.

*

Much later that afternoon they were moving smoothly over the still blue sea towards the mainland.

Avila was thinking that they had passed through a most amazing and unusual experience and had been saved by the God of Delos himself.

It was the Greeks' firm belief that the Island was under a perpetual spell.

They too had been spellbound as they managed to climb up out of the cave through the hole that the Prince had opened in the roof and then opened the door and collected the statue of Apollo to take back with them.

The Prince had carried it to the yacht.

When he had placed it safely in the Saloon, he had put his arms around Avila to say,

"It will stand on the most beautiful Altar that has ever been built for Apollo and he will bless us so that

~122~

we will never lose the happiness we have at this moment and which will be ours for all of Eternity."

It was only as she felt the yacht move out into the open sea that Avila had come back to reality.

The wonder of Delos, the thrill of being kissed by the Prince and knowing that he loved her had made her completely and absolutely forget everything else.

Now she remembered that he had proposed to the Princess Marigold and not to Avila Grandell, the daughter of a country Vicar.

She could hardly realise herself that she was not the Athene who the Prince believed her to be or the beautiful wife chosen for him by Apollo.

As the mainland came into sight, the sun was sinking and the crimson in the sky was reflected on the waves.

For a moment it seemed to Avila that it was like her own blood, bleeding from the heart that must now lose everything that mattered in life.

"You must be tired, my lovely little Goddess," the Prince was saying. "But I have to take you back to Athens because I promised the Ambassador that you would be there tonight so that you would be ready to leave early in the morning."

"How – early?" Avila asked him in a voice that did not seem like her own.

"I think about midday or perhaps an hour before," the Prince answered. "But I promise I will be with you much earlier. We have to make plans about how soon

~123~

I shall follow you to England. I suppose that you will have to ask for the permission of Queen Victoria to marry me."

Avila did not answer.

The agony of what he was saying was almost unbearable.

"You are tired," he said gently. "We will talk about it tomorrow and, of course, when I have followed you to England."

He paused for a moment before he went on,

"I think it would be a mistake for me to travel with you. Her Majesty might think that I am presuming on her hospitality. I know that she is reputed to be very difficult, but I cannot believe that she will not accept me as your husband."

As they drove back in the chaise to Athens after leaving the Prince's yacht, Avila said very little.

She was only acutely aware of the Prince being beside her and her love for him welling up in her heart like a tidal wave.

It was just impossible to think of anything but how handsome he was and how she would love him despairingly to the end of her life.

'There will never, never,' she told herself, 'be another man like him.'

They were late arriving at the British Embassy and by this time it was nearly dark.

It had taken them such a long time to fight their way out of the cave.

When they returned to the yacht, they had to walk so slowly because the statue of Apollo was so heavy.

The British Ambassador greeted them enthusiastically.

"I have been worrying about Your Royal Highness," he spoke to Avila. "If you had not arrived soon, I would have had to send out a search party."

Avila thought to herself how this had very nearly been a necessity.

"I must apologise for being late," the Prince said. "But I will leave the Princess to tell you the story of the very exciting discovery we have made."

"Nobody would be surprised at anything that happens on Delos," the British Ambassador remarked.

Avila held out her hand to Prince Darius.

"Thank you so much for a very – wonderful day. It is a day – I will never ever – forget."

He took her hand in his and kissed it.

Just for a moment they looked into each other's eyes and it was quite impossible to look away.

Then without speaking the Prince turned towards his chaise.

"I have put back dinner half an hour, Your Royal Highness," the Ambassador was now saying, "so you don't have to hurry unduly."

"Thank you," Avila managed to answer.

She had been told before they left that there was to be a party tonight.

She was glad in a way that the Prince was not staying for the party as it would have been difficult, in fact agonising, to have to talk to anyone else when he was there in the dining room.

Avila could not help thinking, when he had walked away from her, that it was the last time she would ever see him. That exactly was what he had to do.

She was halfway up the staircase when she stopped.

"I think, Your Excellency," she spoke to the Ambassador who was still in the hall, "we should arrange to leave early in the morning. Perhaps no later than nine o'clock. I know that Lord Cardiff is very anxious to go back to England as soon as possible."

"He is indeed, ma'am," the Ambassador replied. "I know that he will be very grateful for your thoughtfulness."

"Then you will arrange it, Your Excellency?" the Princess asked.

"Of course," the Ambassador promised. "I will give orders tonight that you will leave here at eight-thirty."

Avila went on up to her room.

As she did so, she knew that darkness encompassed her.

She could no longer feel or see the Light of Apollo.

CHAPTER SEVEN

Avila stood on the deck of the British Battleship watching until Athens was out of sight.

She knew that she was saying 'goodbye' not only to Greece but also to a wonderful and glorious love that she would never find again.

At last, when she could only vaguely see the coastline, she went below.

Her maid had already unpacked and her cabin seemed so empty and, taking off her hat and her jacket, she sat down on the bed.

She was trying to think clearly and not to heed the agony that was in her heart.

'I love – him. *I love – him*!' she kept thinking over and over again.

She felt again the wonder of his kisses and the rapture he had given her yesterday from the moment they had stepped onto the Island of Delos.

As the Battleship steamed on, the sea began to grow rougher.

One of the storms that appear suddenly in the Mediterranean made the Battleship pitch and roll.

Avila was not upset by the sea.

In fact it was a relief to think that now she had an excellent excuse not to go and sit in the Saloon with the Greek Ambassador and Lord Cardiff.

They would expect her to be suffering from sea-sickness and, like Lady Bedstone, had taken to her bed.

All she really wanted was to be alone with herself.

To think over what had happened and to remember every word that the Prince had said to her.

Gradually the agitation she had felt in getting away from the British Embassy before he arrived had subsided.

She then began to think more sensibly about the future.

If he followed her, as he intended to do, he would find on arrival in England that Princess Marigold was married to Prince Holden.

The question then was whether he would return straight back to Greece or whether he would visit Windsor Castle and ask for an audience with the Queen.

And Avila knew that it was extremely important that he should not go to Windsor Castle.

If he asked questions, the Queen might suspect what had actually happened.

Avila wondered what on earth she could do to prevent there being any possibility of this happening.

It was then she remembered with a sense of relief that Prince Holden would be meeting her when she arrived at Tilbury.

Her mother would also be waiting for her, as they had arranged, at *The Traveller's Rest.*

She would then go back to the country with her, never to be heard of again.

'I am grateful, of course, I am very grateful for having seen some of the unique glory of Greece,' she told herself, 'but I know that I will never feel the same again and there will be emptiness in the future that can never be filled.'

That night when she went to bed, the Battleship was still pitching and rolling even more strongly.

However all she could think of was the Prince and she cried herself to a restless sleep.

It was something that she was to do every single night of the voyage.

Because it was so rough in the Bay of Biscay, she was able to stay in her cabin all the time without it causing any comment.

Lady Bedstone sent her messages which she replied to, but otherwise she was alone with her thoughts and her memories.

As they left the Bay of Biscay and drew nearer to England, Avila knew that she must make an effort to join the Ambassador and Lord Cardiff.

The coastline was actually in sight when, dressed in the black gown that she had worn when she came on board, she joined the two gentlemen for luncheon.

They appeared to be delighted to see her.

"We have been very worried about you, ma'am," Lord Cardiff said. "The Captain says he had never known the sea to be so rough, but as you know, this can happen in the spring."

He paused a moment and then continued,

"I have congratulated the Captain on not having lost any time despite the awful weather."

Avila sat down with them and tried to eat a sensible meal.

While she was all alone in her cabin, she had had no wish to eat anything at all.

She only pecked at the food that her Greek maid conscientiously brought to her every mealtime.

Now she told herself that she had to return to ordinary life and behave in an ordinary way.

"I have just been telling Lord Cardiff" the Greek Ambassador was saying, "how much I have enjoyed the visit to my own country, even though it was for the sombre occasion of a funeral."

"I know Your Royal Highness enjoyed it too," Lord Cardiff said, "and I am certain that what Prince Darius showed you of the Greek Islands was extremely interesting and unusual."

"Very – interesting," Avila managed to reply.

"I consider him to be just the right person to be the Guardian of some of the Islands," the Greek Ambassador remarked. "He has always been most knowledgeable about our history and I am quite certain if there are any treasures left on Delos or the other Islands he will find them."

Lord Cardiff laughed.

"I think you are being optimistic. The Islands have been stripped in every century and the French have been the busiest in this plundering."

"That is indeed true," the Greek Ambassador remarked, "and I am so furious at hearing what they have taken from Delphi."

"I don't blame you," Lord Cardiff said. "At the same time, because the statues of Greece are so perfect, they must belong to the world."

The two men then began a somewhat heated argument as to whether the treasures from one country should be taken to another to be displayed in Museums and Art Galleries.

The Greek Ambassador made a special point of claiming in no uncertain terms that the Elgin Marbles should be returned to where they belonged in Athens.

Avila decided that she would stop listening to them.

She was thinking of the unearthly beauty of the statue that she and the Prince had found in the cave.

And she wondered if there were any more under the pile of earth where Prince Darius had stood.

If indeed there were, she knew that she would never see them.

Again she felt the agony of loss, almost as if the statues were her own children.

*

It was in the early afternoon that they finally reached the Port of Tilbury.

As they did so, Lord Cardiff made a flattering speech to Avila.

He told her how much he had enjoyed her company and how splendidly he thought that she had carried out her duties at the funeral of Prince Eumenus.

"I shall tell Her Majesty she could not have sent anyone who would have represented Great Britain better," he said.

"Thank you, my Lord," Avila answered him.

"That is certainly true," the Ambassador chipped in, "and you will not forget, ma'am, that I shall be asking you to honour our Embassy with a visit. I will keep you notified of all the entertainments and parties that take place there."

"I shall look forward to hearing from you," Avila sort of smiled.

As *H.M.S. Heroic* moved slowly into the quay, she went up on deck.

She could not remember what time Prince Holden told her that he would be expecting her and she wondered what she should do if by any chance he was late.

Lord Cardiff and the Ambassador would expect her to be carried away immediately to Windsor Castle in a smart carriage.

She need not have worried.

When she looked down at the quay, she could see that Prince Holden with the Harbour Master were waiting to welcome her.

There were a number of carriages which were to take the different members of the party from the Battleship to where they wished to go.

Prince Holden came aboard.

He cordially greeted the Captain and then the Greek Ambassador and Lord Cardiff, who quickly made their farewells and then hurried down the gangway to the carriage which was waiting to take him back to Whitehall.

Once again he congratulated Avila profusely on the success of her visit to Greece.

He repeated that he knew Queen Victoria would be delighted with the report he intended to give her.

When he had gone, the Greek Ambassador made no move to follow him.

Prince Holden, who had already greeted Avila effusively, now said to her,

"I think now we should be leaving."

"Yes, of course," she answered.

She shook hands with the Captain and the other Officers and thanked them for a pleasant voyage despite the Bay of Biscay.

The Captain responded by saying what a privilege it had been to have her on board the Battleship.

Avila was escorted down the gangway by Prince Holden with the Greek Ambassador following behind them.

Avila then climbed into the chaise and Prince Holden deliberately waited until the Greek Ambassador went ahead of them.

Avila knew that he would undoubtedly think it strange if, having come straight from the ship, he saw them stop at *The Traveller's Rest.*

Finally, as his carriage disappeared out of sight, they then started to drive slowly along the quay.

Lady Bedstone was in a closed carriage behind them and, although she might think it odd for them to stop at the hotel, she would, Avila reckoned, not make any fuss about it.

As soon as Prince Holden had driven the chaise a short distance from the ship, he asked,

"Was everything all right?"

"Everything!" Avila replied.

"No one was suspicious that you were not the Princess?"

"No, not at all, and Lord Cardiff was very complimentary, as you heard just now."

"I cannot tell you how grateful I am to you," Prince Holden said. "But, of course, we must be very careful that no one has the slightest suspicion of what has occurred."

"No one in Athens queried for a moment that I was not who I was – supposed to be," Avila assured him.

Try as she would, she could not help there being just the suspicion of a sob in her voice.

She hoped, however, that Prince Holden would not notice it.

"You have obviously been absolutely splendid." he was saying. "I know that Her Royal Highness has a special present for you to express her gratitude to you and I thought, as you live in the country, you might like me to give you a horse."

"A horse?" Avila exclaimed. "Of course I would love one and it is very very kind of you to think of it, but there is no need for you to give me anything."

"There is every need," he replied. "You have given me happiness and that is something that cannot be bought over the counter."

Avila laughed.

"That is true and I have been fortunate enough to see some of the beauty of Greece."

She wanted to add, 'and unfortunate enough to lose my heart!'

But that was something that no one must ever know.

Prince Holden then drew up his horses outside *The Traveller's Rest*.

"You will find your mother in the same bedroom that you used before you left," he said, "and thank you from the bottom of my heart for being so brave."

Avila managed to smile at him.

Then she stepped out of the chaise and hurried into the hotel.

She pulled the veil over her face and knew that the Proprietor, who was waiting to escort her to the stairs, could not see her clearly.

It was not likely, she thought, that he would notice any difference anyway. Except that she knew she was very different from the carefree girl who had left *The Traveller's Rest* such a short time ago.

She had started out then on what she had thought would be a really exciting adventure.

It had been and so much more and she recognised now that she would never be the same again.

In a way she had grown up.

She was no longer a girl but a woman.

As a woman, she had learnt the wonder and the glory of love and inevitably all the agony and despair of losing it.

The same maid in a mob cap guided her up the stairs.

"There be a lady waitin' for Your Royal Highness," she said.

She knocked on a bedroom door, opened it and bobbed a curtsey as Avila went inside.

She saw her mother standing by the dressing table.

She ran towards her and was then suddenly aware that Princess Marigold was more or less concealed on the other side of the bed.

"Avila, dearest! You are all right?" Mrs. Grandell asked.

"Yes, perfectly, Mama," Avila replied.

She threw back her veil so that she could kiss her mother.

Then turning to the Princess she curtseyed.

"Everything went off perfectly, Your Royal Highness."

"I am extremely grateful to you," Princess Marigold replied.

She was wearing a white summer dress, not unlike the one that Avila had worn when she had arrived at the hotel from the country.

Now she started to change into the black gown that she had brought with her.

It was unpacked and lying on the bed.

"I shall need my bonnet," Princess Marigold said. "I am sure you found the veil useful in case people stared at you too closely."

"Yes, indeed," Avila answered, "and thank you very much, ma'am, for the lovely gowns you put in the trunk. I am sure that His Royal Highness will arrange to have it collected from my home."

She thought that he would do when he sent her the horse that he had so kindly promised her.

"Oh, don't worry about them," Princess Marigold smiled. "If they are of any use to you, do keep them. I hate black and I have enough of it to last for a thousand funerals!"

Mrs. Grandell laughed.

"I am sure, Your Royal Highness, you have been told over and over again that black is very becoming to your fair hair. But thank you for your generosity to my daughter."

"So I shall always be deeply in her debt," Princess Marigold said, "and, although we are unlikely to see each other again, I shall always remember how you helped me at a time when I most needed it."

Mrs. Grandell was doing up the back of her gown as she spoke.

Avila had taken from her head the bonnet with its dark veil and laid it out on the bed and then Princess Marigold sat down at the dressing table to put it on.

As she did so, she declared,

"I know you will be interested to hear that tomorrow my engagement to Prince Holden is being officially announced and we are actually being married in two weeks' time."

"Then, of course, Avila and I want to wish Your Royal Highness every happiness," Mrs. Grandell smiled.

"I would expect that Her Majesty is furious that everything is being done in such haste," Princess Marigold went on lightly, "but I am so afraid that somebody else may die and we are plunged into mourning again that we are taking no chances!"

"I think that is very wise of you, ma'am," Mrs. Grandell said, "and, of course, you have all of our very best good wishes."

"I shall be very happy," Princess Marigold said firmly. "Although Her Majesty may not approve, I am content to have what must be a small Wedding before I leave for my husband's country."

"You will be married, I imagine, at Windsor Castle?" Mrs. Grandell enquired.

"I am afraid so," Princess Marigold replied, "and my bridesmaids will have to hurry to have their gowns made as I shall have to hurry to buy my trousseau."

She was speaking as if the whole thing was rather a joke, which Avila found surprising.

She next rose from the dressing table saying,

"Thank you again, Avila. But you have not yet told me if Greece is as beautiful as you expected it to be."

"It was very very wonderful, ma'am," Avila responded in a low voice.

"Then we have both had very satisfactory holidays," the Princess grinned.

She put out her hand to Mrs. Grandell.

"Thank you for all your help. I most sincerely hope that one day your daughter will be as happy as I am."

She smiled at them both and, as they both curtseyed, she walked towards the door.

When she reached it, she pulled the veil over her face and then slipped out.

Avila knew that Prince Holden would be waiting for her at the bottom of the stairs.

No one would suspect for a single moment that she was not the same person who had just walked up to them.

"Now you must change your gown," Mrs. Grandell said to Avila. "And then we can go home."

Her daughter turned round so that her mother could undo the buttons at the back.

As she did so, Mrs. Grandell said,

"I have missed you, my dearest. Tell me what you thought of Greece."

"It was even more – wonderful than I ever expected it – to be."

"I want to hear everything from the moment you left me here," Mrs. Granclell said, "and, of course, which places you visited in Athens."

For a moment Avila thought that it would be impossible for her to speak of what she had seen and felt when she had been with Prince Darius.

She could remember all too vividly the compliments he had paid her as she gazed at the marble maidens supporting the portico of the Erechtheion.

She could remember every world that he had said the next day when he compared her to Athene and asked her to be his wife.

It was easy to say very little while her mother was helping her to change her clothes.

But it was more difficult when they were driving back home in the closed chaise which Prince Holden had hired for them.

Only by pretending that she was very tired and closing her eyes as if she wanted to sleep did Avila manage to say very little.

She did, however, describe the funeral and the Reception at the British Embassy to her mother in some detail.

"I am disappointed that you could not have stayed in The Palace," Mrs. Grandell said. "It is very beautiful inside and some of the statues it contains are really breathtaking."

"I did not know that you had been in The Palace, Mama," Avila queried in surprise.

"I did not mention it because I thought it was unlikely that you would ever have a chance of seeing it," Mrs. Grandell replied quickly. "Now tell me about the Parthenon."

Avila stammered out a few sentences of praise.

Then, as she recalled the Prince's voice and the nearness of him, she closed her eyes.

The cross-examination was becoming more and more agonising and she could only pray that her mother would never guess how much she was suffering.

Her father was waiting to greet her when she eventually arrived home.

"I hope you have enjoyed your holiday," he said. "Your mother has been worrying about you all the time you were away, but I really cannot think why."

"It was all very exciting, Papa, and it was interesting to see places which Mama has told me about. I know you will be pleased to hear that everyone thought that my Greek was very good."

"How can it be anything else when you have a Greek mother?" the Vicar asked. "Now, thank goodness, you are back. Your mother has been behaving as if you had disappeared to another Planet and we would never see you again!"

Avila managed to laugh.

"I am back," she cried, "and now it will – all seem like a – dream."

This was the truest thing, she now thought, that she had ever said.

Of course it was a dream, a dream so beautiful and so perfect, that it could never come true.

When she was alone in her bedroom, all she could see was the anemones covering the ground in front of her.

All she could feel was the Prince's hand holding hers.

She was vitally aware of the strange Light.

It was different from the light in any place she had been to before.

She wondered too if she would ever know again the mysterious quivering, the beating of silver wings and the whirring of silver wheels.

They belonged to Delos and she would never see Delos again or Prince Darius!

Then the wonder of all those moments would gradually fade away until she doubted to herself if she had ever really been aware of them.

'How can I bear it? How can I go on living?' she asked herself again and again that night.

She threw open the window and looked up at the stars overhead.

They were the same stars that had twinkled above her when she was in Greece, but now they seemed far away and some of their enchantment had gone.

How was it possible that she had been transported to know the ecstasy of the Gods?

And now to be thrown into the dark emptiness of being human?

Suddenly Avila felt the tears running down her cheeks.

'I have – lost him! I have lost – him!' she sobbed into her pillows.

She knew that she had lost not only the Prince but somehow Apollo as well.

She had also lost her soul or perhaps she had left it behind on the island of Delos.

*

Having cried herself to sleep, she woke in the morning feeling that everything was a huge effort.

She just wanted to stay where she was and not have to speak to anyone.

Then she told herself that it would be a great mistake for her father or mother to think that her visit to Greece had not been just a normal holiday.

Having acted the part, she must go on acting now as herself.

She dressed and went downstairs before anyone else was about.

Leaving the house, she walked to the stables.

She could not help hoping that Prince Holden would remember to send her the horse that he had promised.

It was then she recalled somewhat belatedly that the Princess had given her a present just before she left the bedroom.

Because her mother was in a hurry to leave, Avila had not opened it at the time.

She had put it into her handbag and never gave it another thought. It was upstairs in the chest of drawers where she always kept her bag and her gloves.

The horses seemed glad to see her and nuzzled against her demanding affection.

She told herself that when she had had breakfast she would go riding.

That at least she would be able to do alone.

She had always had permission to ride in the Park that belonged to the Duke of Ilchester and it occurred to her then that she had never seen Prince Darius on horseback.

She just knew, however, from the way he drove the chaise and controlled the horses that he would be an outstanding rider.

His horses would instinctively respond to anything he asked of them.

'How can he be so different from any other man?' she wanted to know.

She knew the answer anyway.

He had told her what it was when he said that they had known each other for a million years already.

For the first time she wondered if he would feel incomplete without her.

Then she was sure that it was far too much to ask.

He might seem like a God, but he was also very much a man of the world.

He travelled extensively and held an important post in his own country and owned great possessions.

Moreover he believed that it was Princess Marigold who had visited Athens for Prince Eumenus's funeral.

The Greek newspapers would be sure to carry the story of her engagement and later of her marriage.

When he read the stories, Prince Darius would know that it was impossible for him, as he had wanted, to marry Princess Marigold.

He would doubtless be hurt and offended that she had not told him of her engagement.

The result would be, Avila reasoned to herself, that he would not come to London as he had intended.

He would remain in his own country and doubtless in time would find another woman he would take to Delos. And she too would seem to him like Athene.

Avila wanted to cry out because it hurt her so much to think about it and she continued torturing herself every day and night.

And yet she knew she was being sensible and that was exactly what would happen.

The sooner she accepted the inevitable the better it would be for her.

She left the stables and walked out into the garden.

It seemed to her very small and insignificant.

Although the flowers were brilliant in the sun, they could in no way compare with the masses of anemones that covered the Island of Delos.

"It is over! It is over! It is over!"

She forced herself to repeat these words until she was quite sure that they would go on repeating themselves in her subconscious mind even when she was asleep.

It had been a glorious and magnificent interlude in her rather dull and conventional life.

Now she knew that Prince Darius would not even think of her as a woman he had loved.

She had deliberately kept from him the knowledge that she was engaged to be married to another man.

He would believe that she had been deceitful and that she had lied to him.

That was something she knew that he could never forgive or forget.

Now the pain in Avila's heart was even worse than it had been before.

There was nothing she could do – nothing!

She heard her mother calling for her, which meant that breakfast was ready.

As she walked back to the house, she was saying over and over again in her mind and her heart,

"It is over! It is over! It is over!"

*

The next two days passed slowly, so slowly that it seemed to Avila as if each hour was a century of time.

"I don't know what is the matter with you!" the Vicar said to his daughter. "You seem to me to have had such an exhausting holiday that you need another one to recuperate in!"

"I am – only a little tired, Papa," Avila replied.

Her mother was going to visit someone at the end of the village who was sick and, when she had driven away, Avila went back into the garden.

She knew that she had to make an effort and not loaf about as she had been doing for the last two days.

She walked past the yew hedges and under the trees to where there was a small stream that her mother always referred to as the 'water garden'.

It was very attractive, but for the present moment Avila could see only the blue mist over the Aegean Sea.

She could hear the soft rippling waves lapping against the shore on the beautiful Island of Delos.

She had forced herself fairly successfully not to cry for the last two nights.

Now her unhappiness could no longer be controlled and she felt tears come into her eyes.

Then to her surprise she heard footsteps coming towards her through the garden.

She supposed that her father needed her and so she turned round.

Then she was spellbound.

She thought that she must be dreaming and her heart had stopped beating.

It was not her father who was approaching her through the garden,

But *Prince Darius.*

For a moment when he reached her, they could only stand gazing at each other.

Then he held out his arms.

Without speaking and without even thinking, Avila flew towards him.

He pulled her close to him and his lips came down on hers.

She felt once again as if the whole world was enveloped in a vivid Light.

She heard again the silver wheels moving overhead.

Prince Darius kissed her not gently but possessively until, as had happened in Delos, her body melted into his.

A long time later he raised his head to say,

"How could you leave me? How could you go away without a single word? Why did you not tell me the truth?"

It was impossible for Avila to speak.

She could only stare at him, the tears still wet on her cheeks.

Gently he kissed them away.

Then he demanded,

"Now tell me that you love me!"

"Y- you – know that I – love you," Avila stammered. "B-but – why are you – here? How did you know where to – find me?"

"I knew," he answered, "when you left without telling me you were going, that I had to follow you. I boarded the very next ship, but I arrived in England too late to go to Windsor Castle that night."

Avila gave a gasp of horror.

"You – have not been to – Windsor Castle?"

The Prince smiled.

"Does that frighten you, my darling? Not half as much as it frightened me when I found a strange young woman impersonating you."

Avila was now trembling.

"You – you spoke to – Princess Marigold?"

"When she was told that her visitor had come from Greece, she was sensible enough to receive me alone," the Prince replied, "and the moment I saw her, I knew at once that she was an imposter."

Despite herself Avila could not help giving a little choked laugh.

"You cannot – have accused the Princess of – impersonating me! But – did you not think she was me?"

"Do you suppose for a moment I did not know that, while there was a resemblance of looks, there was something really vital missing that you and I found together on the Island of Delos?"

Avila knew exactly what he meant, but she was still frightened about what further had happened at Windsor.

"Was the Princess – very angry that – you were not deceived – as everybody else had been?" she wanted to know.

"No, and she understood that I had to know the truth, the whole truth, otherwise I might go to the Queen."

"Y-you would not have – done that?" Avila cried.

"I would have turned the whole world upside down to find you!" the Prince declared. "If it meant accusing Queen Victoria of fraud, I would not have hesitated to do so."

"Princess Marigold – must have been very – frightened of you!" Avila gasped.

"She was frightened but intelligent enough to understand that what I wanted was you. So she told me where to find you."

He did not wait for Avila to reply, but kissed her again.

He kissed her until she felt as if she was being carried up into the sky by angels and she was burning in the heat of the sun.

Only when they could breathe again did Prince Darius say,

"And now, my precious one, we are going to be married as quickly as possible so that I can take you back to Greece with me."

"B-but – you cannot – marry me."

"Why not?" he demanded.

"Because you thought you were – proposing to someone who is – Royal like yourself and I am – just very – ordinary."

The Prince laughed and it was a very happy sound.

"How can you be ordinary if you are Athene and given to me by Apollo himself? Come now let's go and talk to your father who I was told is writing his Sermon and so could not be disturbed."

Avila gave a little laugh.

"So the servants – told you to come into – the garden to – find me?"

"They said that Miss Avila was in the garden and I knew that was the little Goddess for whom I was seeking."

"Y-you are not – angry because I – deceived you?" Avila asked him nervously.

"Very angry that you did not trust me, but now I understand it was something you could not do. I was even angrier to think that you could believe you could go away and forget me."

"I would – never have – forgotten – you," Avila replied, "and I have been so desperately unhappy since I – left Athens."

He looked down at her.

"You are thinner and there are lines under your beautiful eyes," he said. "So, Heart of my Heart, I believe you."

"I swear I will never – never lie to you again, but this was not – my lie and incidentally Papa does not – know why I went – to Athens. He just – thinks I was – invited by Princess Marigold to go with her and help her to brush up her Greek on the voyage."

Prince Darius did not speak and she added quickly,

"Please, please – don't – upset him!"

"Do you think I would do anything that would upset you?" the Prince asked. "Now let's go and find your father and tell him that we wish to be married."

They walked towards the house and, as she had done before, Avila slipped her hand into his.

She knew, as a thrill ran through her when his fingers closed over hers, that once again they were one before all the Gods.

It was the same feeling she had had when they were on Delos. Earlier in fact when he had taken her to see the wonder of the Parthenon.

They entered the house and as they did so Avila was aware that her mother had returned.

She was in the drawing room and the door was open.

"Come and meet my mother," Avila suggested.

"That is something I am very anxious to do," Prince Darius answered.

They walked in and Mrs. Grandell, who was standing by the window, turned round in surprise.

"Mama," Avila began, "this is – His Royal Highness Prince Darius – of Kanidos whom I met when I was – in Greece."

She rather stumbled over the introduction.

Then she was aware that Prince Darius was staring at her mother in a strange way.

Mrs. Grandell moved towards him and Avila was aware of a worried expression in her mother's eyes.

As she reached the Prince, he exclaimed,

"But surely I am not mistaken? You are Cousin Lycia!"

"And you are Darius!" Mrs. Grandell said. "I believe that I would have recognised you, although you are older and much bigger than when I last saw you."

Avila looked from one to the other.

"Are you – saying that you know – Mama?" she asked the Prince.

"Your mother is my cousin," Prince Darius explained, "and Princess Lycia was, when she was your age, one of the most beautiful girls in the whole of Greece."

Avila stared at her mother in complete astonishment.

"*Princess* Lycia?" she questioned.

"I have never told Avila what happened," Mrs. Grandell explained quickly.

"I think you would like to know," the Prince said, "that I saw your brother a month or so ago and he said that he often wondered what had happened to you. And now that your father is dead, he intends coming to England to try to find you."

"My brother said that!" Mrs. Grandell exclaimed.

"I think that your whole family feels the same," Prince Darius replied, "just as my family believed that you had been very harshly treated."

"What are you – talking about – what are you – saying? You *must* – tell me!" Avila cried, showing a certain amount of frustration.

The Prince smiled and took her hand in his.

"Your mother ran away with the man she loved," he said, "just as I am prepared, my darling one, to run away with you if your father and mother do not accept me as a suitable husband for you."

"And – Mama ran away– and she is really a – Princess?"

"A very important Princess," Prince Darius replied. "Her father was Prince Alexius of Zacynthos, one of the largest Greek Islands. But he was an exceedingly proud man and was horrified when his breathtakingly beautiful daughter wanted to marry a not very important Englishman – "

"My husband may not have a title," Avila's mother interrupted, "but his family is one of the oldest Saxon families in existence and held Office in the County of Devon long before the arrival of William the Conqueror."

Prince Darius laughed.

"I am only putting it from your father's side," he pointed out, "for he expected you, as you were so beautiful, to marry no less than a King."

Avila's mother laughed too.

"But I fell in love," she said, "with a young man who had just come down from Oxford University and was touring Europe."

"So you – ran away with Papa!" Avila cried excitedly.

"We ran away and my father cursed me for disobeying him. He declared that I was no longer one of his family and he would not acknowledge me as his daughter."

There was a note in her voice that told Avila how it had hurt her.

"He also stripped me of my title and everything I possessed," her mother went on. "But I was completely content, my dearest, just to be your father's wife and your mother."

"No one can understand that better than I can," the Prince said, "for I would marry Avila, as you call her, if she was the daughter of a fisherman. But you will understand it will make things far easier for me and for her when it is known that her mother is Princess Lycia and a cousin of my mother whom everyone loved."

"I loved her too," Avila's mother nodded.

"Your other relatives and there are a good number of them," Prince Darius said, "still love you and will welcome you back home. I promise you that is the truth."

He smiled before he added,

"Now I know why my lovely Avila and Princess Marigold resemble each other."

"Why?" Avila asked.

"The Princess's father, Prince Dimitri of Panaeros," he answered, "was the nephew of your mother's mother."

Avila laughed.

"So I am actually related to Princess Marigold?"

"Yes, you are second cousins and your grandmothers were sisters," the Prince agreed, "but it would be wise not to mention it at the moment, at any rate, not until we arrive back in Greece."

He saw the question she wanted to ask before it reached her lips.

"I would like to marry Avila in Athens," he said to her mother, "and if you agree, we will go there immediately, as I just cannot wait very much longer to make her mine. And we have some very important work to do in Delos."

"Married – in Greece!" Avila exclaimed. "I cannot imagine – anything more wonderful!"

"That is what it will be," the Prince said quietly.

"I must go and tell your father," Avila's mother now insisted.

She ran from the room and Prince Darius drew Avila to him.

"How could we have imagined," he asked, "that our Fairy Story could have such a happy ending?"

"I could not – think it was – at all possible," Avila sighed.

"With Apollo and Athene looking after us," the Prince replied, "everything is possible. That is why, my lovely one, we will be married in Athens and our honeymoon will be spent in the Islands, the most exciting being Delos where we will discover together what else there is hidden in the third cave."

CHAPTER EIGHT

Prince Darius did not tell Avila what he had felt when he went to the British Embassy, as arranged only to find that she had already gone.

At first he could not believe it possible and said firmly to the butler,

"I think you must be mistaken. I understood that Her Royal Highness was leaving later this morning."

"Her Royal Highness left the Embassy at eight thirty," was the reply, "and I understand that the *HM.S. Heroic* sailed promptly at nine o'clock."

If anyone had given him a body blow Prince Darius could not have been more stunned.

He had gone to bed thinking and believing that he had never been so happy.

He had found the one woman in his life, who was the wife who he had always sought.

Princess Marigold he was sure was completely and absolutely the other half of himself and he had always been quite certain that this Greek Legend was true.

The Creator, they related, had divided the human beings He had created because he was lonely.

One half of Him was soft, sweet, beautiful and spiritual, the other was strong, protective and far-seeing.

Prince Darius had set in his heart a shrine that contained the ideal woman who he would marry and be happy with for ever and ever. She would help him with his work in Greece and his protection and interest in the many Islands especially Delos.

Even when he was a small boy Prince Darius wanted to be a Guardian of that particular Island.

Now it was his, he felt as if he had been given the most priceless jewel that the world had ever known.

When he had taken Avila there, he was almost certain that he was right in thinking that she felt as he did.

That the air was alive and the Gods were speaking to them as they had spoken to Apollo.

He had not been mistaken.

He had known with certainty then that his long search was now at an end.

He had found the true love that all men sought and only some were fortunate enough to find.

Yet incredibly she had left Athens without telling him.

Without apparently even leaving a note behind to explain her strange behaviour.

He thought it was beneath his dignity to ask, but he had to know the truth.

"Did Her Royal Highness leave a message for me?" he enquired of the butler.

He shook his head.

"There was no message, Your Royal Highness," he replied.

It was then that Prince Darius knew that he had to find out why Marigold had left.

Could she have really changed her mind at the last moment and no longer cared for him?

It seemed so impossible that he almost laughed at the idea.

He had never been in love before.

Naturally there had been many women in his life. Because he was so handsome and of such importance, they had pursued him ever since he had grown up.

He would not have been human if he had not accepted what had been offered to him so freely.

He knew well that almost every woman with whom he came in contact, looked upon him as the God Apollo.

Yet there was a vast difference between them and Avila.

He confessed quite simply to himself that there had always been an expression in their eyes which he knew was an invitation.

In fact, now he thought it out, he was fully aware of the truth.

Whilst the other women he met looked on him as Apollo the man, Avila looked upon him as Apollo the God.

That he told himself was the difference that he so wanted, the difference he sought and the difference he thought he had found.

It was typical of his quickness of mind that he decided to follow Princess Marigold and learn exactly what had happened from her own lips.

He sent a servant post-haste back to his house to collect his luggage.

He himself went to the docks to find what was the next ship leaving for England from the Port.

He was informed that a large Liner was leaving that evening at six o'clock.

He booked himself the most comfortable cabin available and waited for his servant to join him in Athens.

In the meantime so that no one should be suspicious or interested in his movements, he went back to the British Embassy to see the Ambassador.

He appeared very much at his ease.

He explained to the Ambassador that he had misunderstood the time the English Party was leaving.

It was important that he should have wished Her Royal Highness, '*Bon Voyage*'.

It was then he learnt that it was she who had changed the time of departure and it was entirely her suggestion that the *H.M.S. Heroic* had left so early.

This only confused the Prince more than he was already.

When finally he boarded the Liner he was bewildered in a way he had never been before.

There had been one woman who he had very nearly married and who had been Greek.

Her family was as important as his own and everyone had told him how suitable she was to be his wife.

His relations had almost begged him on their knees to marry her.

It was, they had pointed out to him, extremely important he should have an heir to carry on the family line.

Also it was usual for those of the old and revered families to marry young.

Because they had been so persuasive, he had actually considered this particular choice of theirs more seriously than he had any of the other young women who had been brought to his notice.

She was certainly very lovely and her figure was perfect and her face had been admired by every artist in the country.

'If I have to marry,' the Prince said to himself, 'why not her?'

Finally because she was very much in love with him and he was on the point of saying the four words that would seal his Fate.

Then he thought that he would take her to Delos.

Delos meant so much to him and he so loved going there alone and disliked his friends either criticising or worse still bemoaning the Temples that had been lost or plundered.

They would chatter on and on until he could not bear to hear the same sentences again and again.

To take the woman he was to marry to Delos would he thought be the final test.

If she felt as he always did the very strange air that came from the Gods, then he would most certainly marry her.

He would know for sure that he was doing the right thing.

They had gone to the Island of Delos one evening when the sun was sinking in the sky.

To the Prince the air was alive with mysticism that he could not put into words.

Yet he knew that it was there for those who felt just as he did and were in touch with the Gods.

She looked around appearing to be even more beautiful as the light from the sky haloed her head.

The stars seemed to shine in her eyes and Apollo's Light was everywhere as far as they could see.

Then she said in a slightly artificial voice,

"What a pity this place is in such a mess and everything that was worthwhile has been stolen."

The Prince was then taking her back to the mainland as fast as he could manage it.

Once again he vowed to himself that he would never marry anyone until she felt as he felt in Delos.

All the way when he was travelling towards England he was thinking of how Princess Marigold had quivered against him when he had kissed her.

How she had known then that there was a strange Light glittering and shining in the sky and the air itself felt like a dancing flickering flame.

It was what the Prince had felt and he could read her thoughts.

He knew what she was feeling just by looking into her eyes.

Then she put out her hand and slipped it into his.

As his fingers tightened on hers, he had known she felt a mysterious quivering between them and he felt the same.

He was sure that she had heard, as he did, the beating of silver wings and the whirring of silver wheels.

He remembered how he himself had said to her quietly,

"The God of Light was born here on Delos and the Greeks are perfectly aware of the strange quality of light which illuminates this Island."

"I can – feel it," Avila enthused to him in a whisper.

How could she have invented anything like that? How could she have been anything but absolutely and completely truthful?

Her feelings were his feelings and nothing would ever persuade him that this was not the truth.

All through the turbulent Bay of Biscay and the long run up the English Channel, he was turning over and over in his mind exactly what had occurred.

He was reliving the moment in the cavern when she had flung herself against him as she asked,

"*Shall we really have — to stay here and — die?*"

He had known at that moment that she was his.

When he had bent his head forward and found her lips, he knew that it was something that had been ordained since the beginning of time.

He had found what he had always been seeking.

He kissed her for a long time and felt her body melt into his.

Only when they were both a little breathless did he speak to her.

He could see by the light of the lantern the rapture in her eyes.

No woman could have looked more beautiful and at the same time so spiritual.

No woman he had ever known had looked at him as if he was Apollo the God in whose territory they were standing.

Then the question was back again as to why if she felt like that had she left him?

*

He arrived at Windsor Castle the following morning. He was so early that the elderly *aide-de-camp* was not yet on duty.

It was therefore a young man who had taken his request to speak to Her Royal Highness Princess Marigold straight to her private apartment.

Princess Marigold has finished breakfast, but had not yet sent for Colonel Bassett to cope with her correspondence.

When the *aide-de-camp* had said His Royal Highness Prince Darius of Kanidos desired to see her, she had stiffened.

It was a shock because she had never anticipated that anyone from Greece would follow Avila home to England.

If Prince Darius was talkative, he might well wittingly or unwittingly cause a great deal of trouble.

She had therefore thought quickly and said to the *aide-de-camp*,

"I will see Prince Darius right away and alone. Do not inform my Ladies-in-Waiting that anyone is with me."

"Very good, ma'am," the *aide-de-camp* bowed.

While he was fetching Prince Darius, the Princess moved around rather restlessly.

She was not certain how to compete with anyone who made trouble and she was wishing desperately that Prince Holden was with her.

He would be coming to Windsor Castle later in the morning, but that was of no help at this moment.

The door opened.

"His Royal Highness Prince Darius of Kanidos, ma'am, is now here" the *aide-de-camp* then announced rather pompously.

Princess Marigold was standing at the window and for a short moment because she was frightened she did not turn around.

Then, as the Prince did not speak, she turned slowly so that she was now looking towards him.

Just for a moment she saw an expression on his face that told her what he was expecting.

Then it changed abruptly.

He walked towards her saying:

"I am afraid, ma'am, I have been taken to the wrong apartment. I asked to see Her Royal Highness Princess Marigold."

"I am Princess Marigold," she replied nervously.

"Not the Princess Marigold who came to Athens for the funeral of my uncle?"

"You are quite certain of that?" Princess Marigold asked.

"Completely and absolutely," Prince Darius replied. "Although I do admit that there is a slight resemblance."

Princess Marigold looked towards the door as if she felt that someone might be listening.

Then she appealed to him,

"Please help me and whatever happens you must not say that here."

"Say what?" Prince Darius asked her looking puzzled.

"That I am not – the Princess you – met in Athens," she stuttered.

"Then where is she?" the Prince demanded.

Now there was a note in his voice which told the Princess that he was determined to hear the truth.

"I want your help," she then said. "And please be very careful – what you say."

He sat down on an armchair and Princess Marigold then started the whole story at the very beginning.

She told him how angry she was when she was told that she had to go to Greece because she knew that Queen Victoria was trying to prevent her marrying the man she loved.

She recognised as she explained what she felt for Prince Holden that Prince Darius was becoming sympathetic to her.

By the time she had finished her story he understood exactly why she had behaved as she had.

He thought it amazingly clever on her part that no one had the slightest idea that she had been with Prince Holden when she should have been in Athens at the funeral.

"If you told Queen Victoria," Princess Marigold said, "she would be very very angry. So please understand and go away as quickly as you can."

"I will leave immediately," Prince Darius replied. "If you will please tell me where I can find the person who impersonated you so brilliantly."

Princess Marigold hesitated.

"Why do you want to see her?" she asked him.

"Because I am going to marry her and quite frankly nothing and no one will stop me!

The Princess laughed and it was a happy sound.

"What could be better," she said, "and you will take Avila away to Greece and no one will ever guess for a moment that I might have a double somewhere in England."

"Just tell me where I can find her," Prince Darius insisted, "and I promise Your Royal Highness that neither of us will ever trouble you again, unless, of course, you wish to come and visit us in Greece."

"I might well do that one day," the Princess smiled, "but please promise me that you will not talk to anyone in Windsor Castle before you leave."

"You can trust me," Prince Darius said. "I swear to you that everything you have told me will be shared only with my future wife."

The Princess went to her writing desk and wrote down Avila's address for him.

Then, as she handed it to the Prince, she said,

"You are quite right to fight for what you want, that is what I had to do and I have won. But I don't want any repercussions or reproaches."

"Of course not," Prince Darius agreed at once, "and may I wish Your Royal Highness every happiness in the future."

"And I wish you the same," Princess Marigold said, "and I think, if we both get our own way, we are very lucky people."

"And very persistent ones," Prince Darius grinned.

He left her and hurried to find even faster horses to carry him to the country and to Avila.

When the first excitement of his arrival and his insistence that they should be married immediately had subsided slightly, Avila suggested,

"We must be extremely careful that we do not betray Princess Marigold. As I expect you realise, Queen Victoria would be very angry if she ever found out what had happened."

"I have given the Princess my word," Prince Darius said, "that I would not speak of it to anyone but to you, my darling."

"But supposing when I go back to Athens as myself, people will think it very strange that I look like Princess Marigold."

"Greek families," Prince Darius said, "are very closely related to each other over many years that it is not surprising that quite a number of Greeks resemble each other."

He paused for a moment and then he commented,

"Looking as you do at the moment, my precious, without that heavy black, you might be several years younger than the Princess,"

"I suppose that is a compliment." Avila replied. "If I was several years younger, I would be back in the schoolroom and you might find me very dull and uninteresting."

"I would never do that," Prince Darius said. "To me you are everything that I have ever wanted and I will love you whatever age you are, even when your hair is white."

Avila laughed.

"Then I suppose because you are like Apollo you will never grow old, but always remain the same, a God of Light and Healing and driving across the sky. It is not fair."

The Prince had laughed and pulled her into his arms.

"You are so beautiful, my precious, as your beauty comes from inside rather than out, it will increase and be ever more blinding to mere mortals as the years pass."

"I hope that is true," Avila sighed. "Please love me whatever I am like."

"You can be quite sure I will," he answered.

He then started once again to make arrangements for her father and mother to come to Athens as quickly as possible.

"Avila has to have a trousseau," Mrs. Grandell pointed out, "and that will take time."

"Time is what I cannot allow you," Prince Darius said. "I want Avila with me as speedily as possible. I am going to go ahead merely so that I can arrange that everything is perfect for you. At the same time I am a very impatient bridegroom!"

Both the Vicar and Mrs. Grandell realised that this was undoubtedly the truth.

Then Mrs. Grandell observed a little tentatively,

"My husband will have to ask permission of the Duke of Ilchester to be away, as he is the Duke's Private Chaplain."

She hesitated for a moment and then she added,

"Actually the Duke and Duchess are the only people who knew who I was and where I came from. When my husband was fortunate enough to be offered this position as the Duke's Chaplain and Vicar of the village, he, of course, made enquires as to whom he had married."

Prince Darius smiled.

"I expect he was surprised."

"I rather thought that he might be shocked that I had run away from my family. But, as you understand, I was in love."

"Just in the same way as I am in love with your daughter," Prince Darius added. "I will speak to the Duke and I am sure that everything will be arranged to suit you both."

Next they took him to the Duke's house.

The Duke was delighted to meet Prince Darius, having met other members of his family some years ago.

When he heard that he was to marry Avila, he congratulated him saying,

"She is not only lovely but ever since she was a child, she has been one of the sweetest young girls my wife and I have ever known."

"You will understand," Prince Darius said, "I want to be married as quickly as possible and not to have to hang about being miserable because we shall seem almost at the other ends of the world from each other."

The Duke then replied,

"I do understand and, of course, Grandell can stay with you as long as you want him. I presume that you will wish him to marry you?"

There was a little pause before Prince Darius responded,

"That is what I hope to arrange, but I believe that the Vicar will understand that it will have to be a double Wedding, one here and one in Athens."

He thought that Avila's father might expostulate, but instead he said,

"Of course it would make things much easier if you could arrange that, because I want, above all things, to marry my own daughter."

"Of course," Prince Darius agreed.

Finally after what seemed to Avila to be endless conversation, everything was arranged.

They enjoyed two perfectly happy days riding the Duke's horses and she wanted to show the Prince the countryside she had lived in ever since she had been born.

She loved the way he appreciated everywhere they went and the country people they had met.

She realised that every moment they were together she loved him more than she had the moment before.

She knew too that he felt the same about her.

They had only to look into each other's eyes to talk to each other without words.

When he kissed her, she knew that the wonder and glory that she had felt in Delos was still with them.

At last Prince Darius said that everything had been organised and he must return home.

The night before he left he took Avila into the garden after dinner.

It was still not quite dark although the first evening stars were coming out in the sky.

"Promise me," he insisted, "that you will think about me every moment that I am away."

"I shall be counting every second until I can be with you again." Avila answered.

"I am afraid to leave you," he said putting his arms around her. "I could not go through the agony I felt all the way here when I thought I had lost you and you no longer loved me."

"How could you think that?" Avila said. "I cried every night when I was alone because I thought I would never love anyone again and I would be unhappy for all of my life."

"That is something that will never happen," Prince Darius vowed. "I love you so much, my precious darling, and I swear I will make you very happy."

He pulled her against him and kissed her until she felt that she was a part of him and they could not be any closer.

Then he took her back to the Vicarage.

She went straight up to bed knowing that she would dream that he was still kissing her.

*

He left early the next morning.

Only when the chaise carrying him to London was out of sight did Mrs. Grandell say firmly,

"Now we have a great deal to do and, unless you are going to make your future husband very angry, we shall have to hurry."

It was certainly a hurry to find all the clothes that she would want and to buy the gowns that she felt Prince Darius would admire.

Fortunately there was an excellent seamstress in the village who could alter the gowns they brought from London. Therefore they could buy dresses that were already made.

Only Avila's Wedding dress took a little longer than anything else.

This was because Prince Darius has told her mother exactly what he required.

"It seems a strange idea for the bridegroom to choose the bride's gown," Mrs. Grandell remarked.

"Because I am Greek I understand what he wants," Avila said. "I am sure that he wishes me to look like – one of the great Goddesses."

"Like Athene," Mrs. Grandell replied, "and that is, as you know, aiming very high."

"We must not – disappoint him," Avila insisted nervously.

"I am quite sure you will not," her mother answered.

Finally they set off from Tilbury in a grand Liner that was on its way to India.

Avila could hardly believe that she was leaving England again so soon.

'After this,' she thought, 'I shall be living in Greece and my husband will be Greek and so will my children.'

She was aware as she had never really been before that her mother was very Greek.

She knew as they were approaching the Mediterranean that Mrs. Grandell was worrying about how her family she had left so many years ago would receive her.

She had run away knowing that nothing mattered expect her love and she could honestly say that she had never for a moment regretted doing so.

At the same time she had sometimes felt very lonely for her family and she had longed to see her sisters and brothers again and the friends who she had been brought up with and their families.

She could hardly believe that Fate had moved in such a mysterious manner to take Avila back to Greece.

She had to admit, however, that Prince Darius was the most charming young gentleman.

Only as the ship moved into Port did Mrs. Grandell stand rather close to her husband.

It was as if she was afraid of what might be waiting for her personally in Greece.

The first person to come aboard was Prince Darius.

Avila was waiting for him and, as soon as he stepped on deck, she ran towards him.

He kissed her despite the presence of the Captain and other Officers.

She said in a rapt little voice that only he could hear,

"You have – come! It seems like a – million years until I – saw you again."

"Ten million for me, my darling." he answered affectionately.

Then behind him came a tall good-looking man of about forty years of age.

He ignored Avila and went straight to her mother.

"Welcome home, Lycia," he smiled and kissed her cheek.

Avila saw the tears coming into her mother's eyes as she said,

"Oh. Ptolemy, it is wonderful to see you."

"And to see you back where you belong," her brother said. "I think you should know that your title has been restored officially only this morning and you are now 'Princess Lycia' as you have always been to us."

Mrs. Grandell wiped away her tears.

It was, Avila realised, a moment of overwhelming happiness that her family accepted her again.

She saw that her uncle was now shaking hands with her father and she looked up at the Prince.

"Now everything is all right," she sighed

"Of course it is," he answered her, "because you are here and I am never going to lose you again."

It was something that he made very sure of the following day.

He had arranged for them to stay at the British Embassy and Avila was touched when she learned that she and the Prince were to be married early in the British Embassy Church.

There was to be no one to witness the Marriage Ceremony except for her mother and the British Ambassador.

"You will understand, my darling," Prince Darius said, "that all my family and all my friends who have known me since I was a child would wish to come to the Cathedral."

He kissed her forehead before he went on,

"We will be married according to the Greek Orthodox faith in which we will then bring up our children."

Avila blushed and looked a little shy and he went on,

"We have to do everything together and where we worship outwardly is important to the outside world."

The way he spoke told her without him saying anything more what he was thinking.

She and he together would also worship the Gods that were so very close to them.

Yet officially they must pay tribute to the faith that they had been brought up in.

"You think of − everything," she murmured softly.

His fingers tightened over hers as he said.

"I think of you and nothing else is of any consequence."

When Avila put on the beautiful and sublime Wedding gown that had been made at the Prince's request, she knew that it was a perfect garment for the part she had to play.

It was in a very soft chiffon which was not so popular amongst brides at this moment in time. It clung to her figure and made her appear ethereal and an intense part of the sunshine.

The skirt swept out at the back and made a train of its own.

Over the softness of the gown there was a lace veil made by Greek fingers at least two centuries earlier.

She expected the Prince to lend her some of the superlative jewels that her mother had told her were famous in Greece.

The wreath that came with the veil was of small white lilies and field flowers which she knew grew in such profusion on Delos. And there was a bouquet for her to hold of the same blossoms.

When she entered the Embassy Church to find Prince Darius waiting for her, he thought that she might have stepped straight down from Mount Olympus.

Her father duly married them and Avila was certain that it was a Service they would both savour and remember for the rest of their lives.

Every word he spoke told them that he understood what they were feeling for each other.

Also that the God he worshipped and in which he fervently believed was blessing them as well.

When she rose after the Blessing, the Prince lifted back Avila's veil.

He then kissed her very gently on the lips.

It was a simple kiss not of passion but of dedication.

She knew that he was vowing to protect and love her for the rest of his life.

A little while later Avila drove to the Cathedral with her father.

Prince Darius had already gone ahead of them.

Because everyone in Athens had heard about the Ceremony which was to take place, the roads were lined with people who waved and small children who threw flowers at the chaise.

To Avila it was all very exciting and very moving.

When she stepped out at the Cathedral, the crowds started to cheer and wished her luck as she walked up the stone steps to the West door.

The huge Cathedral was filled with both the Prince's and her mother's relations.

Everybody who knew either of them wanted to be present on this exceptional occasion and be a witness to the ultimate happiness of the young couple.

Every pew was packed and there was a full choir, who sung divinely

The Marriage Service was taken by three Priests dressed in long robes.

To Avila it was a little awe-inspiring, but the Prince was beside her and he made certain that she made no mistakes.

When they walked down the Aisle, those watching thought that no two people could look more radiantly happy.

Outside the Cathedral the crowd had considerably increased since they had gone inside for the Service.

There were cheers as they reached the open carriage that they were to travel back to The Palace in.

Having heard of the marriage, King George had sent a message to say that he was deeply disappointed that he could not be present on such a splendid occasion and that he wished the couple all the happiness in the world.

But he placed his Palace at their disposal for the Wedding Reception.

It was a kind action that considerably endeared him to the Greek people who he was just getting to know.

It was, Avila thought later, a very intelligent thing to have done.

The Palace was very impressive.

The multitude of flowers that Prince Darius had arranged to have displayed everywhere made the air fragrant and aromatic.

There was a huge Reception first to which everyone who had been in the Church was invited.

Then there was a Wedding Breakfast for all the families and relatives.

These amounted to over three hundred and naturally there were speeches from some of the older members. And there was a very amusing and witty reply from Prince Darius.

There was a room set aside in The Palace for Avila to change from her Wedding gown into a going-away dress.

It was particularly attractive with a little hat which was not much larger than the wreath she had worn at the Wedding. She looked lovely yet at the same time very young.

When she said a fond 'goodbye' to her mother, the Princess Lycia was once again nearly in tears.

"Enjoy yourself, my darling Avila," she said. "I know that Darius will take extra good care of you."

"You can be quite certain I will," the Prince chimed in.

They drove away amid more cheers and a cloud of rose petals.

As they went down the street, he said,

"Now we can have the Wedding the way I really want it."

"Another Wedding!" Avila exclaimed in surprise.

"You have been quite marvellous," he answered. "You have said all the right things to the right people and now, my precious one, we will be alone. There is so much I want to tell you and so much that matters only to you and me."

She did not understand, but she was so happy she just pressed her cheek against his arm.

He was driving an open chaise in which he had taken her driving before.

The horses were even faster and she thought even more impressive this time.

They did not talk very much as they left the City of Athens and the houses behind them.

Avila was just happy to be with him.

Then to her surprise instead of going as she had expected to his beautiful house, she saw that they were nearing the sea.

A short while later she was aware that his yacht was waiting for them in a small bay.

She so wanted to ask him questions, but she felt that it would be a mistake.

When they went aboard, the Captain congratulated them on their Marriage and then put out to sea.

The Prince did not take her below as she had thought he would.

They stood on deck and watched until the Islands came into sight.

They seemed to glitter in gold as the sun was sinking in the East.

Suddenly Avila realised that they were going to the Island of Delos.

She did not say what she had just realised aloud, but the Prince then said,

"That is where I thought we should both be and in case you are frightened, my precious one, let me tell you that I have arranged for us both to be very safe even though you will not see who is guarding us."

For a moment Avila was afraid that the man who had shut them up in the cave might spoil the happiness of their night together.

Then she reckoned that the Prince would have seen to everything.

They drew nearer and nearer and then they stopped in a different part of the Island to where they had been on the previous occasion.

There was a small bay with a wooden jetty jutting out on one side of it.

Avila found they could step on to it from the yacht.

The Prince took her by the hand and they walked off the jetty and up a path on to the top of the cliff.

It was then that she saw they were in a part of the Island where there were trees.

The ground was covered with anemones that had been there before and their scent was in the air.

They walked in the shade along what seemed an easy path until suddenly to her surprise, she saw a building.

She was not certain what it was.

But it was something that she had not expected to find on the Island of Delos.

Then, as they drew nearer she saw that it was made with trees and the many branches still had their leaves on them.

The Prince did not speak.

Then when they reached the strange building, he pulled aside a green curtain.

It blended in with the trunks that constituted the walls.

Inside there was a room.

At one end there was a large bed draped with soft muslin curtains.

To her surprise she saw on the other side that there was no wall.

She could then see that there was a large pool on which the last glimmering light of the sinking sun was shining.

She looked at the Prince in surprise and he informed her proudly,

"I built this for you, my glorious one. I knew that tonight of all nights, we should be in Delos where the Gods will be close to us and will bless us for all the years of love that lie ahead."

"How could you – think of anything so – wonderful, my darling Darius.

She could see now that there was a soft carpet on the floor and there were small pieces of furniture that seemed to melt into the background of the tree trunks.

The Prince drew her into his arms.

"We will talk about it later, now I want you really close to me."

He kissed her very gently.

Then he disappeared behind the bed where she thought that there must be another room.

She knew what he wanted.

Quickly she slipped off her pretty going-away dress and put it down on a chair.

She then saw lying on the bed a pretty diaphanous nightgown that must have come from her trousseau earlier in the day.

She slipped into the bed and now her heart was beating and she felt a wild excitement creeping up over her.

From the moment they had set foot on the Island of Delos she had felt again the strange quivers hanging in the air that had been there before.

Outside on the pool the sun had gone.

Now she thought that there would be a reflection from the stars up above.

Then the Prince came into the room.

She heard him, but because she was shy, she could not look at him but continued to stare at the pool outside.

Instead of coming to her as she expected, he began to pull at a rope she had not noticed hanging beside the bed.

With a rustle the ceiling overhead moved slowly back until it almost reached the muslin curtains that fell on either side of the bed.

Now she could see the stars above in the sky.

She gave a gasp and gazed up at them.

Then the Prince was beside her pulling her into his arms.

"Now we have the stars in the sky and the wonder and glory of Delos for our Wedding night," he said.

"How could you – think of anything so – perfect and so – incredible," she asked him.

"This is what it will be, my precious," he answered, "my little Goddess, my wife."

He was now kissing her.

Her eyes, her cheeks and the softness of her neck.

Avila knew that there was a vivid Light shining in the room and the air around them was like a dancing flickering flame.

She could feel her whole body quivering against the Prince.

As he kissed her and went on kissing her, she could hear the beating of silver wings and the whirring of silver wheels.

'I love – you, I love – you,' she wanted to say.

But her heart said it to his heart and her soul to his soul.

As Darius made her his, the Gods of Ancient Greece blessed them both with the dazzling Light of Apollo.

OTHER BOOKS IN THIS SERIES

The Barbara Cartland Eternal Collection is the unique opportunity to collect all five hundred of the timeless beautiful romantic novels written by the world's most celebrated and enduring romantic author.

Named the Eternal Collection because Barbara's inspiring stories of pure love, just the same as love itself, the books will be published on the internet at the rate of four titles per month until all five hundred are available.

The Eternal Collection, classic pure romance available worldwide for all time.